"I'd like to stay for a few days, Kayla. Just in case this intruder tries again. I'd like to stay in the same room he tried to break in to, if possible."

She wished she didn't need Rafe's help, but she couldn't turn down his offer. Her daughter Brianna's safety had to be first and foremost. After all, wasn't that the main reason she'd called him? She'd known he'd take charge.

Keep them safe.

"If you're sure," she said, meeting his gaze. She was thankful Ellen had agreed to stay with them for a while, too, so that she could take Rafe up on his offer.

"I'm sure." He smiled, and suddenly she remembered all too clearly those moments when he'd caught her close in his embrace.

She swallowed hard and glanced away. She could only hope that allowing Rafe to stay wasn't a huge mistake on a personal level.

For Brianna's sake. Or her own.

Books by Laura Scott

Love Inspired Suspense

The Thanksgiving Target
Secret Agent Father
The Christmas Rescue

LAURA SCOTT

grew up reading faith-based romance books by Grace Livingston Hill, but as much as she loved the stories, she longed for a bit more mystery and suspense. She is honored to write for the Love Inspired Suspense line at Steeple Hill Books, where a reader can find a heartwarming journey of faith amid the thrilling danger.

Laura lives with her husband of twenty-five years and has two children, a daughter and a son, who are both in college. She works as a critical-care nurse during the day at a large level-one trauma center in Milwaukee, Wisconsin, and spends her spare time writing romance.

Please visit Laura at www.laurascottbooks.com, as she loves to hear from her readers.

The Christmas Rescue

Laura Scott

Steeple
Hill®

Published by Steeple Hill Books™

STEEPLE HILL BOOKS

Steeple Hill®

Recycling programs
for this product may
not exist in your area.

ISBN-13: 978-0-373-44418-2

THE CHRISTMAS RESCUE

www.SteepleHill.com

Printed in U.S.A.

For the LORD watches over the way of the righteous, but the way of the wicked will perish.
—*Psalms* 1:6

This book is dedicated to my brother Mike, his wife, Karlene, and their daughters, Brianna and Michaela, with love.

ONE

"Mommy? What's that red thing floating in the lake?"

Kayla Wilson glanced in the direction her five-year-old daughter, Brianna, indicated. The bright sunlight reflected blindingly off the water. Kayla squinted and raised a hand to shade her eyes.

Something red bobbed up and down in the water. She shivered. Not something. Someone. A body. A bloated, dead body. Lying face down, partially snagged on the rocky shore of Lake Michigan.

She sucked in a harsh breath and clutched Brianna close, turning her daughter away from the grotesque sight. She fumbled for her cell phone, her fingers trembling as she dialed 911.

"What's the nature of your emergency?" the dispatcher asked.

"There's a—d-dead body floating in the lake, about a mile north of Pelican Point." Kayla didn't like the idea of her daughter listening to the conversation, but there was nothing she could do.

"A dead body?" Brianna echoed in a high-pitched squeak, tightening her grip on Kayla's waist.

"It's okay, sweetheart. We'll be fine," she murmured reassuringly.

"We'll send a squad. Do you have any reason to suspect you're in danger?" the dispatcher asked.

Suddenly apprehensive, Kayla swept a glance around the area. This section of the lakeshore was usually deserted in December. She and Brianna had wandered north from Pelican Point, away from the memorial that had been recently placed in honor of her dead husband, Jeremy.

Her gaze landed once again on the dead body. She was hardly an expert, but considering the decomposition she could see from here, she suspected the body had been in the water for a while.

"No, I don't think there's any danger," Kayla assured the dispatcher.

"I need you to stay at the scene until the officers arrive," the woman informed her.

"We will." Kayla snapped her phone shut and looked down at Brianna, bundled in her bright pink winter coat and hat. "The police are on their way, Bree."

Brianna kept her face hidden against her side, and Kayla smoothed a hand over her pink knit cap. Her daughter had been only three when her father had died in a freak drowning accident when his charter fishing boat was caught in an unexpected storm. On this second anniversary of his death, she'd brought Brianna here in an effort to keep her husband's memory alive. She worried about Brianna growing up without a father.

Lately, her daughter talked about her friends' fathers with a subtle longing in her voice. Kayla knew Brianna desperately wanted a father of her own.

"Do you think he fell off his boat, too?" Brianna lifted her head to ask, her tiny face pulled into a compassionate frown. Kayla grimaced. Unfortunately, instead of sweet memories, they'd stumbled upon a grisly reminder of Jeremy's death. Brianna had obviously made a connection between the dead person in the water and her father's drowning.

"Brianna, we really don't know what happened," she started to explain, and then broke off, when a movement off Brianna's left shoulder caught her attention. She shifted to see better and her eyes widened when she saw a man wearing a brown canvas jacket and a green stocking knit cap. Something about him was familiar, and as she stared at him, recognition dawned.

Greg Landrum. The guy who'd rented a room in her bed-and-breakfast last weekend.

She didn't know where he'd come from, since she hadn't seen any sign of him earlier, but there he stood staring at them. Belatedly, he smiled and waved, as if he'd recognized them, too.

She swallowed hard and waved back, even though she was keenly aware of their isolation. She wished desperately they'd brought Clyde, their cocker spaniel puppy, with them on this venture. Clyde loved everyone, except Greg Landrum. For some reason, Clyde had taken an instant dislike to her guest. At least his constant barking, growling and nipping might have kept Greg Landrum away.

Kayla turned and opened her phone again, pushing the speed dial button for her brother, Alex, hoping desperately Greg Landrum wouldn't walk over to strike up a conversation.

The guy gave her the creeps.

"Hi, Kay. What's up?" Alex asked.

Comforted by her brother's familiar voice, she managed to keep calm. She didn't want to alarm Brianna by letting her fear show. "Hi, Alex. Where are you? Do you think you could come down to meet me and Brianna at the lakefront?"

"Sorry, Kay, Shelby and I brought Cody to the museum in Milwaukee. Why? What's wrong?"

Her heart sank. Just her luck Alex would be out of town. "Nothing really, but Brianna and I were walking along the lakeshore and we, uh, found a dead body floating in the water."

"What? A dead body?" Alex shouted in her ear. She pulled the phone away with a wince. "Where are you? What part of the lakeshore? Pelican Point?"

"Yes, we're about a mile north of Pelican Point. Don't worry, I've already called the police. They're on the way."

"Are you all right? Is Brianna all right?"

"We're fine. But it's a little creepy being out here." She glanced over her shoulder to the spot where Greg Landrum had been standing, but he was gone. Puzzled, she swept a glance over the entire area. Surely she hadn't imagined him.

The distant sound of a car engine drew her attention and she realized Greg Landrum had simply gone back to his car when she'd called Alex. She watched with overwhelming relief as the bright taillights of a small silver car pulled away from the curb and headed south.

She was glad he'd left. Greg Landrum was an odd guy. He'd claimed he wanted to spend some time hiking in the woods, but he hadn't really dressed appropriately for the cold weather and had complained when his new hiking boots caused blisters on his feet. She hadn't been at all disappointed when he'd packed up to leave.

"I'm sorry, what?" she asked, belatedly realizing Alex was waiting for some sort of response.

"What are you and Brianna doing all the way out there? Don't you have guests at the bed-and-breakfast?"

"My next guests aren't due in until tomorrow afternoon sometime." She didn't mention that they were the only guests booked for the rest of the month. After this weekend, she had nothing scheduled until mid-January. No point in burdening her brother and his new wife with her financial concerns.

"I wish I could come out there to be with you." Her brother sounded concerned. She suspected the idea of a dead body intrigued him, since there was a part of him that missed the action he'd seen while working as a DEA agent.

"Don't be silly," she said with false confidence. Actually, now that Landrum was gone, she wasn't nearly so unsettled. "We're fine. I'm sure the police will be here any minute." At least she hoped so. Where were they? What was taking so long?

"All right. But call me if you need anything," he said firmly.

"I will," she promised. She hung up the phone and within minutes, red and blue lights in the distance caught her attention. The police. Finally. "See, Bree? Here's the police."

"The police are going to help us, right?" Brianna asked.

"Absolutely," Kayla promised, tucking her cell phone into her coat pocket. "They're going to find out who that poor person is and what happened to him."

Several police cars pulled up, along with an ambulance and the local coroner. When Kayla pointed them in the right direction, they all headed down to the shore to examine the dead victim. She swallowed hard and turned away when they eventually pulled the body out of the water, not wanting to see too much.

The police officers and the medical examiner spent so much time at the rocky shoreline, talking amongst themselves, that Kayla grew impatient. They'd mentioned wanting to talk to her, but what was taking so long? It was growing late, the sun was already low on the horizon and Brianna was getting antsy. They needed to get home.

Finally, one of the officers approached them, his expression grim. "Ma'am," he greeted her with a polite nod. "I'm going to need some information from you. Can you give me your name and address?"

"Of course." Kayla dutifully recited the information.

"And what brought you here to this section of the lakeshore today?" he asked.

Kayla explained how she and Brianna had come to Pelican Point to visit her husband's memorial and had decided to take a walk up the path along the lakeshore.

"And did you go down to the body? Did you touch anything on or near the body?" he asked.

"No." She couldn't quite suppress a shiver. "I could tell…" Her voice trailed off, as she didn't want to get into gruesome details in front of Brianna. "I could tell the—person was dead."

"Kayla?" A familiar male voice called her name, making her turn around in surprise. For a moment she could only stare in shock when she saw Rafe DeSilva striding toward her, handsome as always dressed in his crisp navy blue coast guard dress uniform. His normally bright smile had been replaced by a concerned frown.

"Uh, hi, Rafe," she greeted him awkwardly, trying

to ignore the erratic leap of her pulse. Why she reacted so strangely around him, she had no idea. Rafe was a friend of her brother, Alex, and far too attractive for her peace of mind. She'd loved Jeremy and she had no business thinking about how handsome Rafe looked. Besides, Rafe wasn't at all what she was looking for in a man. If she ever married again, and that was a very big if, she'd pick someone stable. Dependable. Not someone who was gone all the time. Like Jeremy had been. She smiled uncertainly. "What are you doing here?"

"Alex called. He was worried about you." He raked a glance over her, as if reassuring himself she was unharmed and then smiled down at Brianna. "How's my favorite five-year-old?"

"Mr. Rafe!" Brianna greeted him with an enthusiastic hug which only made Kayla's scowl deepen. Her daughter had taken to Rafe from the first moment they'd met, and she had no intention of encouraging the friendship. The last thing she wanted was for Brianna to be hurt. "I'm glad you came. We founded a dead body in the water."

"I heard," he murmured, giving Brianna a brief hug, before glancing up at Kayla. "I'm sure that was quite a shock. Are you both all right?"

"We're fine," she assured him, feeling a bit foolish. There was no reason for Alex to have called Rafe. Obviously, she hadn't done a good job of covering up her fear. She turned toward the police officer. "Is there anything else you need? I'd like to take my daughter home."

"Yes, we're finished here," the police officer said, stepping back and closing his notebook. "I don't have any more questions and if I need anything further, I know where to get in touch with you."

"Thank you," she murmured.

"Do you have an ID on the victim?" Rafe asked.

The officer's expression turned impassive. "We have a strong suspicion based on his shoulder tattoo, but we won't release a name until we have a positive ID and next of kin has been notified."

Rafe glanced down at the group down by the lakeshore, as he nodded slowly. "I understand."

Kayla wondered if Rafe knew more than he was letting on. But she'd had enough of hanging around the gruesome scene. She took Brianna's hand and glanced up at him. "We need to get going, Rafe. I'm sorry Alex called and made you come all the way down here for nothing."

Rafe turned toward her with a gentle smile that made her feel incredibly warm despite the definite chill in the air. "Checking on you is never a waste of time, Kayla. Where's your car? I'll drive you back."

"It's not far, just a mile or so down the road," she protested, unwilling to put him out any further.

"I'll drive you," Rafe repeated, steel lining his words. She sighed, recognizing that tone. He'd used it before, a few months earlier, when he thought she and Brianna were in danger from the man who was after her sister-in-law, Shelby. Rafe had gone into protector mode back then and she'd learned that when Rafe made up his mind to do something, there was no dissuading him. Arguing was futile.

"If you insist," she agreed, forcing a smile. She wished she was immune to his charm, but she wasn't. Her normal cool logic seemed to fly out the window around Rafe. Thankfully, she wouldn't have to endure his presence for long. The drive to Pelican Point's parking lot wasn't far.

But the way Brianna gazed adoringly up at Rafe

caused the muscles in her stomach to clench in warning. Fatherless Brianna was more susceptible to male attention than Kayla liked to admit. Especially now.

She couldn't help thinking that with Rafe's lethal charm, even five minutes could be too long.

Rafe escorted Kayla and Brianna down to his jeep, which he'd left parked on the road, but he couldn't help glancing back at the group huddled around the dead victim, his mind buzzing with questions.

He believed with instinctive certainty the police knew the identity of the victim. And he couldn't help thinking he knew who the dead person might be, too.

The prime suspect in his current investigation was Bill Schroeder, the owner of a charter fishing operation out of Pelican Point. Schroeder had been missing for the past week. Long enough for Rafe to fear their suspect was dead.

He'd kept his investigation a secret from Alex because of Kayla. Her husband had once been Schroeder's partner, but since Jeremy Wilson had died two years ago, they'd pretty much ruled him out as being involved in the most recent criminal activity.

His team at the coast guard had been watching Bill Schroeder for the past few months, searching for proof that the owner of the charter fishing business was involved in an underground criminal escape ring, secretly whisking well-known criminals out of the United States through the Great Lakes into Canada—complete with new identities.

If Bill Schroeder was really the dead guy floating in Lake Michigan, then their investigation would take a serious hit. They had a few other potential suspects, but none as promising as Schroeder.

He glanced at Kayla and Brianna once they reached his jeep. He opened the passenger door for them. "Kayla, I need to go back and talk to the police for a minute. Will you wait for me? Please?"

Kayla flashed a puzzled frown but nodded. "I wouldn't mind a ride, since darkness comes so early now. But if you could hurry, I'd appreciate it. I'm sure Brianna is hungry."

Relief washed over him. He was afraid she'd insist on walking back to her car. He turned on the jeep's ignition and cranked up the heat. "I'll be quick, I promise. Five minutes."

He took off at a jog, retracing his steps until he'd reached the group down at the lakefront. He was glad he was wearing his dress uniform when he approached the police officers. He pulled out his official coast guard ID. "I'm Chief Petty Officer Rafe DeSilva, and I have reason to believe this body may be linked to a Coast Guard investigation. You mentioned a tattoo, do you mind if I take a look? If you have a possible identity, I'd like to know."

The uniformed officers exchanged wary glances, but then shrugged. "The tattoo on this guy's shoulder is consistent with a missing person report we received for a William Schroeder. But since there's not much left of this guy's face or his fingers we'll need either DNA or a dental match to be certain."

Rafe's gut clenched.

Bill Schroeder. Just as he'd feared.

He reached down to lift the sheet covering the body and looked at the shoulder tattoo for himself. He had a whole file on Bill Schroeder and he wasn't surprised to see the tattoo of an anchor and the name Jeannie written along the bottom. Jeannie just happened to be the name of Schroeder's ex-wife.

"Thanks," he said to the police officers as he covered the body back up. "We'd appreciate a call once you do have a match with the dental records."

"Sure," the officer agreed.

Rafe jogged double-time back to the jeep to find Kayla and Brianna waiting patiently for him. He slid into the driver's seat and glanced back at Brianna. "Did you time me?" he asked in a light, teasing tone.

"Yep. Mommy helped. You were gone six minutes. You're late," she said matter-of-factly.

He couldn't help but laugh as he put the car into gear and then pulled away from the curb. "You're right. I'm late. Sorry."

"Mom promised we could stop for pizza on the way home," Brianna announced. "Would you like to come with us?"

"Ah, Mr. Rafe is dressed for work, sweetheart," Kayla quickly interjected. "Maybe another time, hmm?"

Kayla's not so subtle un-invite bothered him. He sensed Kayla wanted to avoid him and he wasn't sure why. He didn't think it was because of his Hispanic heritage, although he supposed anything was possible.

He'd never approached her on a personal level, asking her to go out with him. Kayla was a widow, and he was a widower. She was strong and brave and beautiful, but the last thing he wanted or needed was a ready-made family.

He also knew that her brother, Alex, had found God and faith thanks to meeting his new wife, Shelby, but Kayla hadn't. So even though he knew he should stay far away from Kayla and her adorable daughter, he found himself wanting to help in any way he could.

Was it God's intent that he help show Kayla the way? Maybe. At the very least, they could be friends.

"Actually, I had just finished with my meeting when Alex called," he corrected smoothly. "And pizza sounds great. My treat."

Kayla bit her lip and glanced away. He sensed she wasn't thrilled with the idea of him coming along, but he had no idea why. It was just a simple meal.

"Yay!" Brianna shouted happily. He grinned, glancing at her in the rearview mirror. At least one female didn't mind sharing dinner with him.

He ignored the pang of loneliness. The coast guard was his life; he wasn't interested in anything more. His family had been gone for almost five years now. Stranded in the middle of the snowstorm, waiting for the ambulance to arrive, he'd ended up holding his pregnant wife, Angela, in his arms while she and their baby both died from a rare complication during labor.

No, a family wasn't for him. He shook off the sad thoughts as he pulled up in front of Kayla's SUV. "Which pizza place?" he asked.

"DiVinci's," she answered. The restaurant was located in the small town of Bear Lake, not far from where her bed-and-breakfast was located. He didn't doubt she'd chosen the place closest to her house to dissuade him from going.

Ha. Fat chance. He could be stubborn, too. Besides, he couldn't shake the protectiveness he felt toward her. Going to DiVinci's would provide a good excuse for him to make sure she made it home without incident. "Sounds good. I'll follow you there."

Brianna jumped out of the backseat. Kayla leaned on the open passenger door. "Really, Rafe, I can explain to

Brianna. I know you have much better things to do with your free time."

He raised his eyebrows. Did she imagine he had some sort of active social life? If so, nothing could be farther from the truth. "Kayla, relax. I'm hungry and DiVinci's has great pizza. It's just a friendly dinner."

"Okay, suit yourself," she muttered before shutting the door behind her. He watched as she helped Brianna into her child safety seat, before sliding in behind the wheel. He pulled out behind her, following her to the highway.

As he drove, he mulled over the threads of his case. With Bill Schroeder's death, their investigation would halt in a dead end. Schroeder had been their best chance at breaking the criminal trafficking ring. They'd focused their attention on Bill Schroeder in the first place because one of the local police officers had spotted Bruce Pappas, a well-known criminal awaiting trial, down at the lakeshore getting into one of Bill Schroeder's boats. After that, Bruce Pappas had suddenly vanished. Never showed up for his court date. And had never been seen again.

At the time, Schroeder had insisted he'd returned Pappas back to shore, and the authorities had never been able to prove otherwise.

So they'd begun keeping Schroeder under surveillance. They'd noticed he took trips at odd times during the day and night. But while his actions were suspicious, they needed hard, irrefutable proof. They'd been hoping to catch him in the act of actually transporting a criminal, but so far they'd had no luck.

So much for that plan.

He called his young partner, Evan Marshall, and his commanding officer Luke Sanders, to give them the news. Sure, they'd have to wait for a positive ID, but clearly it looked as if Schroeder's disappearance had been the result of foul play.

Neither man answered their phones, so he left messages and then snapped his phone shut with a sense of frustration. Not that it really mattered that Evan and Luke didn't answer, there was nothing more they could do tonight anyway. They'd need to regroup and find another thread to follow in the investigation.

He pushed thoughts of work aside with an effort. He needed to focus on relaxing and enjoying himself for once. He couldn't remember the last time he'd had dinner with an attractive woman.

Of course this wasn't a date, he hastily assured himself. Just a nice dinner with a friend and her daughter.

When Kayla turned into DiVinci's parking lot, he pulled in right beside her. As they walked inside, he caught a whiff of her strawberry shampoo and had to stop himself from actually leaning closer to breathe deeply, filling his head with her wholesome scent.

He pulled his scattered thoughts away from dangerous territory. He'd promised her a friendly meal, nothing more.

Brianna chatted throughout dinner, which was nice since Kayla was unusually quiet. Brianna explained all about her school Christmas party and the shopping they'd done earlier that day before going off to visit her dad's memorial.

Her last comment piqued his interest. This was the first he'd heard of a memorial. He glanced at Kayla, oddly disappointed. He'd heard from Alex how she'd taken Jeremy's death very hard. She obviously still carried strong feelings for her dead husband even though he'd been gone for two years. He'd been a part of the team that had searched for Jeremy Wilson when his boat hadn't returned to shore. They'd found him, but too late. "That was a really nice idea, putting up a memorial in your husband's memory."

Kayla's smile was strained. "Actually the memorial was Bill Schroeder's idea, not mine."

A prickle of fear raised the hairs on the back of his neck. Bill Schroeder? Had she kept in touch with him over the years? In the months they'd been watching Schroeder, they'd never seen Kayla down by the lakefront near his business. And according to Alex, Kayla hadn't stayed on close, friendly terms with the guy, either.

But she had been at Pelican Point today. On the same day Bill Schroeder washed up along the lakeshore. Not that he believed she had anything remotely to do with his death.

Still, he didn't like the strange coincidence. Didn't like it at all.

Ice formed along the length of his spine. Was it possible Kayla was more closely involved with Bill Schroeder than he'd realized?

TWO

"Did you know him?" Kayla asked abruptly, when Brianna left them alone to greet one of her friends from school dining at a nearby table.

"Who?" he asked, reigning in his chaotic thoughts. "The guy in the water?"

She frowned and nodded. "Yes. I figured you went back to talk to the police because you knew him."

He hesitated, not sure what to tell her. He wouldn't lie to her, but at the same time, he wasn't at liberty to discuss his case. Especially when Kayla happened to know his key suspect on a first name basis. "It's possible the dead guy could be involved in one of our investigations, but we won't know for sure until we have positive ID."

"I see," she murmured, idly toying with the paper sheath from her straw.

He leaned forward, capturing her gaze with his. "Kayla, I need to ask you something. Just how well do you know Bill Schroeder? I mean, I know he was your husband's partner in the charter fishing business, but do you still see him? Talk to him?"

She shrugged. "Not really. He did come over about

a week and a half ago to show me a picture of Jeremy's newly erected memorial."

Ten days ago? Right before the guy disappeared? He tried to sound nonchalant. "Really? What made him think of putting up a memorial after all this time?"

She shrugged. "I'm not sure, I asked him that, too, and he told me he'd always planned on doing it, but just hadn't had made the time. I thought it was a really nice gesture."

Rafe wished he could be so sure. He wanted to ask more, but knew that if he persisted in asking questions, Kayla would grow suspicious. "A very nice gesture," he agreed lightly.

Brianna chose that moment to skip back to their table, so he carefully changed the subject. When they'd finished their meal, he boxed up the leftovers and paid the bill.

"Thanks for dinner, Rafe." Kayla's smile was lop-sided and didn't quite reach her eyes.

"Yeah, thanks for dinner, Mr. Rafe. That was the bestest pizza ever!"

Brianna's exuberance made him grin. "You're welcome, *mi nina*."

Outside, he slid the leftover pizza box in the front seat of Kayla's car while she buckled Brianna in the back.

"I'll follow you home," he said when Kayla climbed behind the wheel.

"That's not necessary, Rafe. I appreciate everything you've done, but you've already gone out of your way for us."

Her sincere gratitude warmed his heart. Startled by the abrupt stab of longing, he took a step back. "Humor me, okay? It's on the way home."

Kayla rolled her eyes. It wasn't on the way, seven

miles in the opposite direction to be exact, but she nodded before closing the door.

Kayla's bed-and-breakfast was located just a few miles west of town. Her home was nestled deep in the north woods, far from the bright lights of the city. Total darkness surrounded them as they drove down her long, winding driveway.

There was a light on in the kitchen, but the rest of the house was dark. He got out of his jeep and came up beside her as she helped Brianna jump down from her perch in the backseat. "Did you set the security system?" he asked.

"Yes."

"Good." He took the pizza box from her hands and led the way up to the front door. Her dog, Clyde, must have heard them because he started barking.

The white panel of the security system was easy to see against the dark exterior. But the green light that normally showed the system was turned on wasn't lit. He frowned. "Are you sure?" he asked sharply. "Because it's not on now."

Kayla stared uncertainly at the security panel, searching back through her memory. "I'm almost sure I set the alarm."

"Okay, take Brianna and go back inside the car and lock the doors," Rafe commanded. "Give me your keys. I'll go through the house."

After everything that had happened, she could only nod, fiercely glad that Rafe had insisted on following her home. "Come on, sweetie," she said, tugging Brianna close. "Let's wait for a bit in the car."

"Why, Mommy? What's wrong?" Brianna's green

eyes were wide with fear as she sensed the tension between the adults.

"Nothing is wrong," she reassured her daughter, not wanting Brianna to be afraid in her own home. "Mr. Rafe just wants to make sure everything is fine before we go in."

"I want Clyde," Brianna said plaintively.

The sounds of the dog barking actually reassured her. She couldn't believe someone was hiding inside with Clyde home. The one thing their puppy was really good at was creating a ruckus. "He's with Mr. Rafe and I'm sure they'll be out soon." Kayla watched through the windshield as Rafe flipped on the rest of the lights, making his way through the inside of her spacious home.

She bit her lip, trying to remember. She had set the security system, hadn't she? She was almost certain she had, but couldn't be absolutely positive. She'd resented her brother and Rafe for insisting on installing the alarm system nine months ago, but lately she'd been glad to have the extra protection. She'd fallen into the habit of using the security system on those days and nights that she and Brianna were home alone. On the nights they had guests, there was no point in using it because her guests could obviously come and go as they pleased.

The elderly couple who'd been her last guests had left this morning, and she and Brianna had left shortly thereafter. It was possible she'd forgotten to set the security system.

Besides, if someone had breached the system, wouldn't the police have been notified?

Rafe returned a few minutes later with Clyde, their clumsy puppy, at his heels. She opened the car door when he approached and climbed out.

"I didn't find any—ah—anything," he said, with a quick glance at Brianna. She was grateful he hadn't blurted out how he'd been searching for an intruder. "But you might want to check things out for yourself to make sure nothing has been disturbed."

"I'm sorry, I must have forgotten to set the alarm," she said softly.

"Probably," Rafe agreed. "The system is set up so that it sends an alarm if the wiring is cut."

That's what she'd thought. "So the only way someone could get past my system is if they somehow figured out my code."

Rafe scowled. "Yes. Do you change it every few weeks like I told you to?"

"I've changed it," she said a little defensively, brushing past him to head up to the door. "Maybe not every few weeks, but I have changed it."

"Check things out. I'll be in shortly," he said, heading over to rummage in the back of his jeep.

"Brianna, bring Clyde inside," she said. Kayla kept Brianna close as she did a quick walk-through. The house was eerily silent. Normally she loved being out in the middle of the woods, far away from civilization, but for some reason the silence bothered her now. Maybe she was still unnerved by finding a dead body in the lake. She glanced around, looking at her things. From what she could tell, everything was exactly the way she'd left it.

Her apprehension drained away. Rafe hadn't found anyone. Everything was fine. She was silly to be so anxious. Obviously she'd forgotten to set the alarm.

"Brianna, it's time to brush your teeth and get ready for bed."

Her daughter groaned, but headed toward their private rooms off the back of the kitchen.

She took the leftover box of pizza and shoved it into her empty fridge. The night out had been an extravagance she really couldn't afford. It was very nice that Rafe had offered to pay. And now she and Brianna would have leftovers tomorrow night, which was a good thing, considering her cash reserves were pitifully low.

She tried to shrug off the gnawing concern. She'd figure out something. She always did.

"Kayla?"

Rafe's husky voice sent her pulse skyrocketing into triple digits. She took a deep breath to steady her nerves before turning toward him. "Yes?"

"Come here. I'd like to show you something." He reached for her hand and the warmth of his touch sent a tingle of awareness up her arm.

He shut off the living room light and she was momentarily blinded by the darkness. "Come outside for a minute, but watch your step."

Curiously, she followed him outside. When he shut the door, she could see the small green light glowing from the keypad, indicating the system was engaged.

Rafe's presence was noticeable, even in the darkness. He stood close. Too close. She eased back a step.

"Your passcode is 7724, right?" he asked.

She sucked in a harsh breath. "How did you know?"

He turned a switch and her porch was awash in a strange, purple glow. He aimed the black light at the keypad. "See how this black light picks up the little bit of oil residue from your fingertips? I could tell the numbers you used were 247 but I didn't know which order. It didn't take me long to figure it out, especially since

I knew you were born in 1977. It may take a stranger a little longer, but not much. Once they have the three digits, it narrows down the possibilities immensely."

Speechless, she could only stare at the evidence he'd presented. He was right. Again.

He tapped in the code and then opened the front door and walked back inside the living room, turning the lights back on. "That's why I told you to change your passcode every couple of weeks. To prevent anyone from figuring it out."

"I never realized," she murmured, sobered by his brief experiment. Her earlier fears came rushing back. She couldn't hide her apprehension. "Do you think it's possible someone was here?"

He paused for a moment, and then slowly shook his head. "No, I don't. If the intruder was smart enough to crack your code to gain entrance to your home, he'd certainly be smart enough to engage the alarm again when he left. Why advertise he was here? I believe you forgot to set it."

She let out a sigh of relief. "You're right. I'm just being silly. And I will change the code, I promise. And I'll clean the keypad regularly, too, as an added measure. Thanks for checking things out for me."

Rafe hesitated at the door, gazing down at her, his expression troubled. "Maybe I should stay. I don't like the thought of leaving you and Brianna all the way out here alone."

Her breath congealed in her throat and she didn't know what to say. Having Rafe nearby would be pure torture, and she wasn't sure her nerves could handle the stress. And Brianna would only get more attached to him than she already was. "I don't think that's a good idea," she said finally. "And besides, you work tomorrow, don't you?"

His intense gaze was mesmerizing, his brown eyes so dark they were almost black. "Yes, but at least I could make certain you're safe here tonight."

"We'll be perfectly safe," she said with more confidence than she felt. "I'm expecting guests tomorrow and they'll be staying through the weekend. I have lots to do to get ready. Really, we'll be fine."

He stared at her for a long moment, before finally nodding. "All right. But promise you'll call if you need me. Do you have my number?"

She hoped he didn't notice the embarrassed flush in her cheeks. Taking his number seemed so—intimate. But when he waited expectantly, she pulled out her cell phone. "No, I don't. But I'll program it in now. What's the number?"

Rafe recited his cell number and she quickly entered the number into her phone. She wouldn't call him, of course, but knowing he was within reach if for some strange reason she did need him was oddly comforting.

"Good night, Kayla." He reached up and tucked a strand of her hair behind her ear. The slightest brush of his fingertips on her skin made her shiver.

She took a step back, plastering a smile on her face. She kept her tone light. Friendly. "Bye, Rafe. Drive safe." When he left, she closed the door and then leaned against the wooden frame, her legs weak. She really had to figure out how to get a grip of her emotions around him. After all, he was just a man.

"Mommy? I brushed my teeth." Brianna skipped into the living room, glancing around. "Where's Mr. Rafe?"

"He had to go home," she said, straightening away from the door.

Brianna's face fell. "But he forgot to say goodbye."

Her heart twisted in her chest before it plummeted to her stomach. This was exactly why she couldn't call Rafe. Brianna already cared about him, too much.

"I'm sorry, sweetheart." She gave her daughter a hug. "He must have been in a hurry to get back to work. Come on, it's bedtime."

"I wanted Mr. Rafe to tuck me in." With a dejected pout, Brianna allowed her mother to take her back to their private rooms. Clyde followed, jumping up on the bed next to Brianna. He'd been sleeping with her since he was an infant puppy and there was no breaking him of the habit now.

She tucked Brianna in bed and gave her a hug and a kiss before shutting off the light and closing the door. Back in the kitchen, Kayla kept busy making a grocery list of the bare essentials she'd need for her weekend guests.

But even as she worked, she couldn't keep her mind off Brianna's keen disappointment. She'd known her daughter had been hinting for a father. Brianna had gone so far as to ask why Kayla didn't go out on any dates like her friend Sophie's mother did. She'd tried to change the subject, but Brianna seemed to have a one-track mind.

Going to the memorial hadn't spurred questions about her dead father, as Kayla had hoped. Apparently, Brianna was more interested in trying to replace Jeremy with someone new.

And Kayla was very much afraid that Brianna might have picked Rafe as a potential candidate to be her new father.

* * *

The next night Kayla tumbled into bed, exhausted after getting her guests settled in. It seemed like mere seconds later when a sharp scream pulled her from a deep slumber.

She leaped out of bed, stumbling in the darkness as she sought and found the light switch. She winced and shielded her eyes from the harsh brightness that flooded the room.

The sound had come from upstairs. She opened Brianna's door to make sure she and Clyde were all right, and then headed down the hall, through the kitchen and into the great room. Her guests, two married couples, were coming down the stairs from the second-floor loft.

"I'm telling you, I saw a man trying to get into our room!" The older woman, Gloria Hanover, spoke in a shrill voice.

"I didn't hear anything," her husband, Edward, muttered.

"I'm so sorry," Kayla said, hurrying forward. "Did you already call the police? Or should I?"

Gloria shook her head no.

"I already checked out their room," Allen Russell said, rolling his eyes. Apparently he wasn't too impressed with Gloria's claim. His wife, Lorraine, went over to stand close to his side. "There's no one there. And even if there had been someone there, I'm sure her shriek scared him off."

"Are you insinuating I'm crazy?" Gloria demanded, facing Allen, her face flushed and her hands propped on her ample hips. "Because I know what I saw. There was a man standing there, his face pressed against the patio door."

"There now, no one is calling you crazy," her husband, Edward soothed, patting her arm.

Kayla tried to smile, but deep down, a cold fear settled in her stomach. Each of the guest rooms had access through a patio door to the deck outside. And she couldn't help remembering how the security system had been turned off. "I'm calling the police. If Mrs. Hanover saw a man, then we need the authorities to investigate."

Leaving her guests to talk among themselves, she went back toward the kitchen to find Brianna standing there with the dog at her feet. She rushed over to give her daughter a hug.

"What happened, Mommy?" Brianna asked sleepily.

She didn't want to scare her daughter, especially after all the strange events over the past two days, but she couldn't lie to her, either. "One of the guests heard a scary noise so I need to call the police."

Luckily, Brianna didn't ask too many more questions. Kayla set her down and made the call. The sheriff's department promised to send a deputy right away. Since everyone was up, Kayla brought coffee, tea and the pastries she'd planned for breakfast that morning to the great room. Playing hostess helped soothe her frayed nerves.

Had her guest really seen a man? If so, who?

The deputy's investigation didn't take long. He took her upstairs to the wraparound deck. Jeremy had designed the house so that every guest room had access to the balcony outside. The deputy pointed with a grim look. "See these gouges? Looks like someone did try to get in."

She swallowed hard, unable to tear her gaze from the

evidence. Apparently Mrs. Hanover hadn't been imagining things at all. Someone had actually tried to break in.

"I'll file a report," the deputy continued. "Could be just a random burglary unless you have reason to believe someone has targeted you, specifically."

"Not that I know of," she said faintly. As much as she wanted to believe in the random burglary theory, the sick dread in her stomach wouldn't let up. What if someone had targeted her? She couldn't imagine why, but the thought wouldn't leave her alone. She forced herself to go back downstairs to where her guests were waiting.

"Edward, I want to leave right now," Gloria Hanover was saying. "I'm not staying here another night."

"Great, just great," Allen Russell muttered.

Kayla's heart sank, but she didn't protest. How could she blame them for wanting to leave? They'd been woken up from a sound sleep by a burglar.

"I won't charge you for last night's stay," she informed the couples graciously. She'd been depending on their fees to help her sagging bank account, but there was no way she could see taking their money. Not after this.

Dawn was beginning to peek over the horizon as the two couples packed their bags and trooped out the door. After they left, she set her security system and then sank down at the kitchen table, propping her aching head in her hands.

What should she do? Why had someone tried to break in? None of this made any sense.

She desperately wanted to call Rafe. Maybe she was overreacting, but as a single mother alone with a young daughter couldn't help being worried. She had an awful feeling there was something significant behind this recent break-in. There had been too many odd things happening lately.

And she wouldn't be able to relax until she understood exactly what was going on.

On Saturday morning, Rafe returned home to review the plans he and his partner, Evan Marshall, and his commanding officer, Luke Sanders, had made the day before.

They only had a couple of thin leads to follow up on. They needed a break in the case, big-time. There was no point in continuing their surveillance on Schroeder's business, considering the local police had Schroeder's boats taped off as a precaution in case it was a potential crime scene.

He and Evan had agreed to split up the duties in their attempts to jump-start the investigation. Evan's job was to begin a preliminary surveillance on Karl Yancy, the recluse who'd taken up residence near Pelican Point, renting a boat slip conveniently located right next to Schroeder's charter fishing business. Yancy had showed up on their radar because of his timely appearance in Pelican Point, the same week as Bruce Pappas's sighting on Schroeder's boat. The coincidence of his showing up when a well-known criminal had escaped was too much to ignore.

Evan's theory was that Yancy was involved too, working with Shroeder. No one seemed to know much about the stranger since he didn't socialize with anyone around the lakefront. And his background information was sketchy, in that it was almost too clean. Which was suspicious enough in itself. So Evan also agreed to do more digging to see what they could find out about the guy.

Rafe's job was to work on getting information out of Charlie Turkow, the grizzled, older man who had a charter business that was in direct competition with Schroeder's. They'd spent some time watching Charlie's charter, too, and had seen some of the same sort of suspicious activity, his boats coming and going at odd times of the day and night.

But when they'd dug deeper, they'd discovered Charlie had a daughter who lived in Michigan. Sure enough, the next two times they were able to follow him, that's where he'd gone. Still, his commanding officer believed Charlie Turkow knew more about what might be going on in Pelican Point than he was letting on and wanted Rafe to uncover whatever the older man knew.

Rafe had swung by Charlie's charter after leaving the gym earlier that morning, but the older man wasn't anywhere around and one of this boats was gone. Since finding him in the open water of Lake Michigan wasn't likely, he returned home. And stewed over what little he knew about Bill Schroeder's activities before he'd died. It bothered him that the guy had gone to visit Kayla. That he'd recently mounted a memorial in honor of her husband's memory.

He raked a hand through his hair.

He didn't like the idea of Bill Schroeder being anywhere near Kayla. Leaving her alone Thursday night had been difficult. At least he could rest a little easier, knowing she had guests staying with her this weekend.

But what about once her guests were gone? She and Brianna were all alone in the middle of the woods.

His cell phone rang, and his chest tightened when he Kayla's name on the display. He couldn't imagine she'd call unless it was important. "Kayla? Is everything all right?"

"We're both fine," she said quickly, as if knowing he might be imagining the worst. He tried to calm his racing pulse. "But Rafe, someone tried to break in last night."

"Break in?" he echoed, jumping to his feet. "Why? What happened?"

"I don't know," she said, sounding truly bewildered. "I had guests, so I didn't have the security system on. But now I'm worried. My guests left early and I changed my access code, but what if the burglar tries to break in again? I'm scared, Rafe."

The underlying fear in her voice gripped him by the throat. "I'm on my way," he said, heading out to his jeep. "Make sure the alarm is set, and I'll be there as soon as possible."

THREE

The fact that Kayla didn't argue worried him even more. Rafe shut his phone and started the jeep, more shaken than he cared to admit. He headed for her house, pushing the speed limit as much as he dared.

Someone had tried to break into Kayla's home. What had the intruder been looking for? Had he missed something the night they'd found the security system turned off? Somehow it didn't make sense that simple burglars would target a home so far away from town.

He'd been a fool to leave her alone.

His cell phone rang again. "DeSilva," he answered, when he saw Luke Sanders' name light up the screen.

"The medical examiner has finished the autopsy on your dead body. The base of his skull was cracked, and the ME confirmed he was dead before he hit the water. Because of the location of his skull fracture, the medical examiner is leaning toward a homicide. The pathology results won't be back for thirty days."

"Did they confirm his ID with dental records?"

"Yes. With the tattoo they were pretty certain he was Bill Schroeder and finding his dentist wasn't hard. He doesn't have a lot of family, so the police are heading out to inform Jeannie, his ex-wife, now."

Rafe grimaced. "I'm sure that will be difficult."

"Did you talk to Charlie Turkow yet? He must know something about the criminals being smuggled out through Canada."

"Not yet. He wasn't around when I stopped in. I'll talk to him as soon as I can."

"All right. Call me if you get something significant."

"Will do." Rafe hung up the phone and tapped his fingers on the steering wheel thoughtfully. Should he let Kayla know about Bill Schroeder? The news was better coming from him than through the media. And he was fairly certain Schroeder's death would make headlines, especially since the medical examiner would likely deem his death a murder.

Rafe pressed a little harder on the accelerator. He couldn't explain this desperate need to get to Kayla. He hadn't felt this protective toward a woman in a long time. Since Angela.

He tried to tell himself to relax, but his lead foot was ignoring the message. When he pulled into Kayla's driveway, he was amazed to note he'd made the trip in a record thirty-three minutes.

The instant he stopped, the front door popped open and Kayla stepped out. His first instinct was to yell at her for not waiting with the alarm set.

But when she hurried down to meet him, he couldn't speak. Instead, he leaped from his jeep and threw caution to the wind, pulling her close in a warm, reassuring hug. "Are you all right?" he murmured, filling his head with her light, strawberry scent.

She grasped him tightly around the waist, burying her face against his chest. "Yes," she said in a muffled voice. "Thanks for coming."

"You couldn't have kept me away," he assured her. Holding her close was sheer heaven. He would have been happy to stay like this all day, but of course, she pulled away when Brianna and Clyde bounded out of the house, followed more slowly by an elegant-looking older woman with silver hair. He recognized her as Kayla's mother-in-law, Ellen Wilson, whom he'd met earlier that year when he and Alex had insisted on putting Kayla's security system in place.

"Mr. Rafe!" Brianna heedlessly flung herself at him and he sucked in a quick breath and caught her before she could get hurt. He lifted her into his arms as the dog barked excitedly at his feet. "You forgot to say goodbye," she accused, looking him directly in the eye.

"I did?" He frowned, distracted by her accusation. He cast his mind backward in time, wondering what she meant.

"The night we had pizza." Brianna's green eyes were full of reproach. "You didn't say goodbye."

"I'm sorry, *mi nina*," he murmured. "You're right, I guess I forgot." He glanced at Kayla who watched their interaction with a worried frown.

"Brianna, I explained how Mr. Rafe needed to get back to work," Kayla said, walking back to the house. Still carrying Brianna, he followed on her heels. "Remember? He works all different times of the day and night."

He wasn't used to anyone making excuses for him. In fact, he hadn't even considered the idea that Brianna would notice he'd left without saying goodbye. He could see by Kayla's guarded expression that he'd inadvertently hurt her daughter.

It was clear she was worried her daughter might be growing too attached to him. And could he blame her?

Brianna was at a vulnerable age. He took a deep breath and tried to collect his thoughts. Brianna was a great kid, but he wasn't ready to be a father again.

Not when he'd failed so miserably last time.

He hadn't been able to save his infant son's life. To have another child dependent on him was inconceivable. The very thought shook him to the core. No, having a family was not an option.

"Next time," he promised, quickly setting Brianna back on her feet and closing the front door behind him.

"Rafe, you remember my mother-in-law, Ellen, don't you?" Kayla said, belatedly reintroducing them.

He cleared his throat and nodded. "Yes, ma'am. Nice to see you again."

"Nice to see you, too," Ellen said, although her expression was guarded and he wondered if Kayla's mother-in-law viewed him as some sort of threat. As if he was trying to replace Jeremy in Kayla's heart. He was tempted to reassure her he'd only come to offer protection, not to start something he had no intention of finishing.

They all walked into the house and Kayla reengaged the security system once they were safely inside.

"Come on, Brianna, we need to finish making Christmas cookies," Ellen said, as if sensing the two adults needed to talk alone.

"Cool!" Brianna raced toward the kitchen, but then paused to glance back at him. "Don't leave without saying goodbye," she reminded him.

"I won't," he promised. He turned toward Kayla. "Tell me about the break-in. What happened?"

Kayla walked over to the sofa in front of the great room fireplace. He froze. She'd put up Christmas decorations. The brightly lit tree in the corner of the room reminded him of his early years with Angela. She'd loved Christmas.

Now there was only a black hole in his heart.

He took a seat across from Kayla, trying to shut out the memories.

"I had two couples staying here last night," Kayla began. "In fact, they were supposed to stay for the weekend. At four in the morning, one of the women screamed, waking everyone up. She claimed a man's face was pressed up against the patio door in her room. We called the police and the deputy found deep gouges in the wood near the door handle where the burglar must have tried to jimmy the lock in his attempt to get in."

"Why didn't you set the alarm on the security system?" Rafe asked.

"Because I don't want my guests to think the alarm is necessary. Business is slow enough without insinuating this place isn't perfectly safe. And besides, it would be too easy for one of the guests to trigger the alarm. All they'd have to do is to open a patio door to let some air in. I refuse to impose restrictions on my guests."

She was right. He didn't like it, but she was right. He remembered she'd argued this point fiercely when Alex insisted on putting the system in.

"I just don't understand. Why would anyone try to rob me? Everyone knows I don't have a lot of money or jewelry or anything else of value."

"I agree, it doesn't make sense," Rafe admitted.

Kayla worried her lower lip between her teeth and he wished there was some way to reassure her he'd keep her safe. "I keep coming back to that strange guest I had, Greg Landrum. He rented a room from me last weekend."

He raised a brow curiously. She hadn't mentioned the guy when they spoke the other day. "Why was he strange?"

She lifted her shoulder. "Little things about him were odd. Like he claimed he had come to hike, but his hiking boots were brand-new and gave him blisters. He didn't have warm winter outdoor gear, either. I heard him making noise in his room in the middle of the night, and when I asked him about it the next morning, he claimed he had trouble sleeping."

"What did he look like?" Rafe asked.

"I don't know, in his mid-thirties maybe, with dishwater-blond hair. He had weasly eyes."

Weasly eyes? "Was that what bothered you? His eyes?"

She frowned. "Maybe. Clyde didn't like him, either. He barked and growled at him all the time. I guess the strangest thing of all was that I saw him down at the lakefront the day Brianna and I found the body." She looked troubled as she gazed at him. "Rafe, do you think it's possible he's targeted me for some reason?"

Greg Landrum. Would be worth putting his name through their database to see what popped. "Maybe, but again, it doesn't make sense that he would come back after he'd already been a guest here. He would know there weren't a lot of valuables here, wouldn't he?"

Unless he was looking for something that only had value to him. But what?

"Yes, you're right." She gave a dejected sigh. "Maybe the deputy was right, that this was nothing more than a random attempt. I don't live in town, but it's possible someone saw the article in the paper and figured I had something here worth stealing."

"Article?" he echoed sharply. "What article?"

She grimaced. "I did an interview for the *Green Bay Gazette* about two weeks ago. The editor is a friend of Ellen's and did the interview as a favor."

He hadn't seen the article and her theory was plausible. He wanted to link everything back to Schroeder, but he could be overreacting. It was possible her break-in had been a random attack. "Do you have a copy?"

"I have several," she responded dryly. "Everyone in town saved one for me. I'll be right back."

He watched her disappear into the kitchen, returning a few moments later with the folded newspaper in hand. Must have been some favor, or a really slow news day, because her picture was plastered on the front page of the lifestyle section. Kayla looked beautiful, her smile a little sad, as she stood in the kitchen. He noticed there was another glossy picture on the wall behind her in the photo. This one showed Kayla and her husband standing down at the marina in front of a charter fishing boat. He scanned the article. It briefly mentioned Kayla's husband, Jeremy, had finished building the B and B in the months before he died. But otherwise, the article was all about Kayla and her renowned breakfast pastries.

"Nice article," he murmured. Broaching the subject of her dead husband for the first time, he raised his gaze to meet hers. "I'm sorry for your loss, Kayla."

"Thank you."

He knew it wasn't really any of his business, but he couldn't help adding, "I know what it's like to lose someone you love. I don't think I would have been able to cope if not for my faith. God's strength and love helped me through the grief."

"Your faith?" Her gaze darted to the cross he always wore around his neck, a gift from his mother after his wife and unborn child had died. "Now you sound like

Alex and Shelby. Alex has changed a lot since meeting Shelby. And he seems very happy."

"Does that surprise you?"

She flushed again and glanced away. "A little. But in a good way. He's a better person now that he's met Shelby. They've invited me to attend church with them, but weekends tend to be my busiest time. At least, when I actually have guests," she amended.

"I understand. When I'm out on the water and attending service isn't an option, I just find a few minutes of quiet time to pray or maybe read my Bible."

"I've never read the Bible," Kayla murmured. "To be honest, I have trouble understanding why God would take my husband away so young."

"Sometimes it is difficult to understand God's plan. Reading the Bible can help. The book of Psalms is my favorite. 'The Lord is close to the brokenhearted and saves those crushed in spirit.' That quote is from Psalm 40:1."

"Sounds beautiful," Kayla said thoughtfully. "Maybe you're right. I'll think about it. Might be interesting to see what has Alex so enthralled."

He wanted to offer to attend church with her, but sensed she wasn't quite ready. Besides, being at church with Kayla would feel like having a family.

Friends, he reminded himself. They were just friends.

Kayla tapped the newspaper article, her attention centered once again on the burglary attempt. "Do you think this article is the cause of the break-in?"

"Maybe," he said, but he didn't really think so. The odd guest she'd had was more concerning. "I think we'll do some digging on Greg Landrum. The fact that he was down at the lakefront when you and Brianna were there bothers me."

Kayla frowned and shivered. "He bothered me, too. I really wanted Clyde with us down there to help keep him away. Which reminds me, did you find out the identity of the victim yet?"

He let out a long breath. This was the moment he'd been dreading. He slowly nodded and reached out to take her hand in his, sure she'd be shocked when he told her the news. "Kayla, the victim you found happens to be someone you know. We've identified him as Bill Schroeder."

Kayla blanched, unable to believe she'd heard him correctly. "Bill? *Dead?* Are you sure?"

"I'm sorry, but yes. We're sure. The police are notifying his next of kin as we speak."

"H-how did he die?" she asked, her voice barely above a whisper.

"His skull was cracked and he was dead before he fell in the water." Rafe's expression was full of compassion. "You need to know, the medical examiner believes he might have been murdered."

She gasped, images from the lakefront scene flashing before her eyes. The red shirt bobbing in the water had been Bill Schroeder. And he'd been murdered? How? Why? "But I just saw him a week and a half ago."

Rafe tightened his fingers around her hand. "I know. You mentioned that the other night. You said he came over because of the memorial. Did he come over here often?"

"Rarely. Maybe more so in the beginning," she corrected herself. "In those first few weeks after Jeremy's death, but not lately. Frankly, I was surprised to see him."

Seeing Bill Schroeder had dredged up memories better off forgotten. The arguments she and Jeremy had over the long hours he worked in the charter fishing business. She'd been thrilled when he'd finally agreed to sell out his half of the business to Bill. She'd been looking forward to more family time.

She rubbed her aching temple. Why was she suddenly remembering the rough points in their marriage? Jeremy had been a good husband and father. She'd never worried about him straying. She'd planned to spend the rest of her life with him.

But Jeremy was gone. All she had left of her marriage was this house, her memories and the memorial that Bill Schroeder had recently put up in honor of Jeremy.

"You knew, didn't you? That's why you went back to talk to the police."

"I suspected, but I couldn't say anything until we knew for sure."

Kayla's shoulders slumped. It didn't matter if Rafe knew before or not. She was doubly glad she hadn't gone down to the body to take a closer look.

"So tell me, how much do you charge to rent one of your rooms?" Rafe asked, abruptly changing the subject.

Startled, she glanced at him. Why was he asking? Because he planned to stay? As much as she wanted to laugh off his offer, she couldn't. Especially now that she knew Bill Schroeder was dead. "Just so happens I'm running a half-price Christmas special," she weakly joked.

Rafe didn't so much as smile. "I'm serious, Kayla. I'd like to stay for a few days. Just in case this intruder tries again. Put me in the same room he tried to break into, if possible."

She wished she didn't need Rafe's help, but she couldn't turn down his offer. Brianna's safety had to be first and foremost. After all, wasn't that the main reason she'd called him? She'd known he'd take charge.

Keep them safe.

. "If you're sure," she said, meeting his gaze. She was thankful Ellen had agreed to stay with them for a while, too, so that she could take Rafe up on his offer. Ellen had mentioned needing to go and visit her sister, who'd fallen and broken her hip, but she wasn't planning to leave until closer to Christmas.

"I'm sure." He smiled, and suddenly she remembered all too clearly those moments when he caught her close in his embrace.

She swallowed hard and glanced away. She could only hope that allowing Rafe to stay wasn't a huge mistake on a personal level.

For Brianna's sake. Or her own.

Rafe left Kayla's house, after making her promise to set the security alarm, so he could run back home to pick up what he needed. Leaving her alone, even knowing Ellen was there with her, wasn't easy. He couldn't help hurrying, unwilling to give Kayla time to change her mind. He'd been shocked at how easily she'd agreed with his plan to stay.

Which only indicated just how scared she'd really been.

He'd returned home to get some clothes and his laptop computer. Once again, he swung by the lakefront, but there was still no sign of Charlie.

He called Luke to tell him about Schroeder's surprise

visit to Kayla days before his disappearance. "I'm going to try to convince Kayla to let me go through her husband's belongings. I just can't help but think it's odd that Schroeder suddenly put together a memorial for her husband two years after his death."

"I'll give you until Monday," Luke reluctantly agreed. "But if you don't have anything by then, I'm pulling you back here. We need to figure out who killed our key suspect. Obviously, someone else must be taking over duty of transporting our crooks out of the country."

"That's fine." Rafe was willing to take what he could get.

When he returned to the bed-and-breakfast, Kayla seemed nervous, as if having him as a guest felt awkward. He used work as an excuse to retreat to his room, where he began an Internet search on Greg Landrum. Thankfully, Kayla had a wireless router for Internet access for her guests.

She invited him to join them for dinner and he warily agreed, trying to come up with some way to avoid giving Brianna the wrong idea.

But when he went down to the kitchen, he found Kayla and Ellen were alone. "Where's Brianna?" he asked.

"She was invited over to her friend's house for a sleepover," Kayla admitted. "I thought it might be best, just in case this guy decides to come back tonight."

Rafe hesitated, abruptly doubting the wisdom of his plan. "Maybe you should both leave, too. You could stay at Ellen's place. I plan to keep the security system off so I can catch this guy in the act." And what he really hoped was to have a few minutes alone with the guy to find out what in the world he was searching for.

"Don't worry about us," Ellen said in a feisty tone. "We'll be fine, right, Kayla?"

Kayla nodded. "We'll keep our doors locked, don't worry. I'm sure I won't be able to sleep much, but I'm staying."

Rafe couldn't think of an argument that would encourage the women to leave, so he fell silent. Kayla served a big pan of lasagna for dinner and made-from-scratch garlic bread. He took a bite and the tangy sauce melted in his mouth. He'd never tasted anything so good.

"You're an excellent cook, Kayla."

"Thanks." She flushed at his praise and then glanced guiltily at her mother-in-law. "Ellen taught me a lot. And it's nice to have friends to cook for, rather than strangers." The subtle loneliness underlying her tone wasn't lost on him. He knew only too well how difficult it was to spend evenings alone.

"Speaking of strangers, I haven't found much on your guest, Greg Landrum," he said, quickly changing the subject to a safer topic. "You told me the address on his driver's license was from Chicago, right?"

She nodded. "Yes. Why?"

"I can't seem to find him anywhere, that's all." He stood to help her clear away the dishes, but Ellen shooed him away, taking over the task herself. "I'm going to keep looking. Everyone leaves some sort of electronic trail in today's world."

"Go on then, we can clean up here," she said. "I have some sewing that needs to get finished tonight, anyway."

"I thought you gave up doing alterations?" Ellen asked over her shoulder.

"No, why would I? Helps pay the bills in the gap between guests."

He stared at her for a moment, hating the thought of Kayla struggling to make ends meet. Doing alterations couldn't possibly pay much. She'd mentioned her bed-and-breakfast business was slow, but he hadn't realized just how serious she'd been.

Was she in danger of losing her business? He hoped not.

"Good night, then. Don't forget to lock your doors. And keep your cell phones close at hand." He was glad Kayla's private living space was tucked in the back of the house, far from the guest rooms.

He wished there was something he could do to minimize the danger.

"We will. Good night, Rafe."

He spent several hours working on his laptop, still not coming up with much on Greg Landrum, although he did find that the guy owned a computer software business in a small suburb outside Chicago.

The information was somewhat reassuring. Greg Landrum did exist, but without a picture, he couldn't be sure that he'd found the right guy. He wanted proof that the man who'd rented a room from Kayla was really Greg Landrum.

When his eyes blurred from the strain of reading his computer, he stretched out on the bed, lightly dozing. The minutes ticked by agonizingly slow.

A soft thud woke him. He levered upward, wide awake. Someone had landed on the wraparound balcony outside. Each of Kayla's guest rooms had access to the balcony, but he'd figured the intruder would come to the same door he'd pried open before. And he'd guessed right.

Sliding from the bed, he slipped soundlessly over to

the door, pressing himself against the wall. He hoped and prayed the guy would come in.

God answered his prayers. Slowly, the patio door eased open. There was no shrill alarm, as he'd purposefully kept the security system off. Rafe held his breath, trying to peer through the darkness.

A figure dressed in black stepped into the room. Rafe waited another beat for the intruder to come in farther so he could grab him. But the figure instantly spun away and Rafe suddenly understood why.

The intruder was wearing night vision goggles and saw that Rafe was in the room.

No! He couldn't let him get away! Rafe followed after him, barreling through the doorway and across the deck.

Rafe took the same path as the intruder. He leaped up onto the edge of the deck railing and then grabbed the low-hanging tree branch. The bark was rough against his palms as he swung to the ground. He ran after the suspect dodging through the trees. The way the branches slapped him in the face had him wishing for the benefit of night-vision goggles.

With only a sliver of the moon for light to guide him, he ignored the stinging pain as he tore through the darkness. Rafe couldn't see the intruder but he could hear him as they both wove a zigzag path through the woods. He thought he was only a few feet behind the guy but suddenly, he heard a rumble of a car engine.

No! Rafe burst through a line of trees at the end of Kayla's property just moments too late. Bright red taillights were disappearing down the highway.

He'd lost him.

Bending over at the waist, he rested his hands on his

knees and took a moment to catch his breath. So close. He'd been so close.

But then he stood, his expression grim. One thing was for certain, the average burglar didn't wear night-vision goggles to break into a house.

And he'd left Kayla and Ellen alone.

He turned and jogged back through the woods, retracing his steps to the bed-and-breakfast. The guy had to be looking for something. But what? Something Kayla had or something someone else had planted? Someone like Schroeder, who'd been there just ten days ago?

Rafe quickened his pace, suddenly anxious to get back.

Whatever the intruder was looking for, he and Kayla needed to find it.

FOUR

Footsteps on the deck had woken Kayla from her light doze. She jumped out of bed and quickly pulled on her robe. She took a moment to peek in on Ellen, who was sleeping, before hurrying out to the great room. Through the large picture window, she saw Rafe disappear into the woods.

Had someone tried to break in? Rafe was obviously chasing someone. The intruder? Fear gripped her by the throat as she stood, uncertain as to what she should do. Call the police? Or just set the security system and wait for Rafe to return?

And what if Rafe didn't return?

The last thought spurred her into action. She grabbed her phone and quickly dialed 911. Thank heavens she'd let Brianna stay at a friend's house for the night.

After notifying the police, she paced the length of the great room, feeling helpless and somewhat vulnerable. It was late, four o'clock in the morning, almost the exact same time frame as the last time the burglar had tried to break in. A coincidence? Or was the intruder the same man? She wrapped her arms across her chest, shivering in the cold.

Rafe burst into the clearing just seconds before sirens split the air.

She ran over to open the door for him. "What happened?"

"I lost him."

She caught a glimpse of his face in the porch light. "You're bleeding!"

"I'm fine." He swiped his arm across his forehead. The blood smeared over his brow. "Scratched by tree branches, that's all."

She couldn't be too disappointed that Rafe had lost the intruder. Not when Rafe had made it back safe and sound. As the sirens grew louder, she confessed, "I wasn't sure what you wanted, but I did call the police."

He shrugged and nodded. "It's fine. We should report the attempted break-in, although I don't think it's going to help. This isn't a simple burglary attempt."

"It's not?"

"No." Rafe glanced outside and she turned to follow his gaze, noting that the sheriff's deputy was already pulling up to the house. "I'll explain more later."

She went over to greet the deputy, a different one than the guy who'd responded to the break-in two nights ago. She tried to smile. "Good morning, Deputy."

The sheriff's deputy did not return her smile. He looked a little annoyed, as if he had better things to do than to respond to her calls. "You reported another break-in attempt?"

"Yes, I did." Kayla glanced at Rafe for help.

Rafe stepped forward, introducing himself and using his coast guard ranking. "I'm staying up in one of the guest rooms, and saw a man trying to break in. I took off after him, but I lost him. There was a car on the road waiting for him. I didn't get the license plate number."

"You took off after him?" The deputy's scowl deepened. "You realize he could have been armed and we could right now be searching the woods for your body, don't you? You're a little outside your jurisdiction. Next time, leave the police work to the experts."

Kayla frowned, about to jump to Rafe's defense, but he put a hand on her arm, squeezing it in warning to keep silent.

"You're right, sir," he said solemnly. "I wasn't thinking. Next time, I'll call you first."

The deputy glared at Rafe, as if sensing he was being humored but then he turned toward the staircase. "All right. Show me which room you were staying in."

Kayla remained downstairs as Rafe led the deputy up to the scene of the break-in. Anxious for something to do, she headed into the kitchen to start a pot of coffee.

The sheriff's deputy didn't stay long. After he left, she handed Rafe a warm moist towel for his cuts. "I guess you were right. There isn't much they can do to help, is there?"

Rafe took the towel and plastered it over his face, wiping off the blood. "No, I'm afraid not. Kayla, the guy who tried to break in tonight wasn't your average burglar. He wore night-vision goggles and had a flashlight strapped to his belt. He came here to find something specific."

She gapped at him. "Like what?"

"I'm not sure. But I have to tell you, I believe these break-ins are related to Schroeder's death."

"I don't understand," she whispered, taking the bloodstained towel from Rafe's hands. "Why would burglar attempts be related to Bill's death?"

Rafe blew out a breath and glanced toward the kitchen. "Is that coffee I smell? Because I could sure use a cup."

"Yes, of course." Kayla turned and led the way into the kitchen, pausing long enough to toss the stained dish towel into the laundry room, before heading over to the coffeemaker.

When the carafe was full, she poured two large, steaming mugs and carried them to the oak picnic table she used for family gatherings.

Rafe took a seat across from her, wrapping his fingers around the mug. She noticed his hands were scratched, too, although not as badly as his face. "I can't explain everything, Kayla, but I will tell you what I can."

She lifted her coffee mug, eyeing him over the rim. "Okay. I can accept that."

Rafe took a bracing sip of his coffee. "We've been watching Bill Schroeder for the past few months. He disappeared about a week ago, and we feared something bad had happened to him. Which is why I wasn't too surprised when he turned up dead."

She stared at him, her own coffee forgotten. "Why was the coast guard watching Bill?"

Rafe's mouth thinned. "Because Bill Schroeder happens to be a key suspect in our investigation."

"Suspect?" She paled. "In what kind of investigation?"

He seemed to pause, as if deciding how much to tell her. "Criminals are being smuggled out of the area, specifically from Chicago, Milwaukee and Detroit, up into Canada. Somewhere along the way, they're also being provided new identities." He took a deep breath and met her gaze head on. "We have reason to believe

Schroeder's charter fishing business was really a front for this underground criminal transportation service."

Rafe braced himself, expecting her to be outraged, but Kayla only stared at him without saying a word. But then the coffee mug began to slip from her fingers, spilling hot liquid over her slender, pale hands. She caught the mug before it fell, but she didn't utter a sound, as if she didn't notice the burning. He jumped up and grabbed a dish towel for her hands.

"How long?" she asked in a whisper. "How long has the charter fishing business been a front for criminal activity?"

The red splotches covering the silky skin of her slender hands worried him. "Come here, we need to run your hands under cold water." He practically dragged her over to the sink, thrusting her hands beneath the cold stream. "We don't know how long. We've been watching Schroeder for the past four months."

She tolerated the cold water for several long minutes before finally pulling away. "Four months? So Jeremy couldn't have been involved. He's been dead for two years."

He wanted to agree, if only to give her some peace of mind, but he couldn't. Because he didn't know for sure that her husband had been innocent. Or if his death had really been the result of an accident. They'd found Jeremy's boat adrift in the middle of the lake after the storm, and within two days, Jeremy's body had washed up along the shore. Jeremy had drowned. No one really knew for sure what had happened. He took a dry towel out and wrapped it gently around her hands. "We don't know," he repeated.

A spark of anger flashed in her brilliant green eyes. "I

know, Rafe. Jeremy would never be involved in anything illegal. Never."

"I'm sure you're right, Kayla, although it is possible Jeremy didn't know what was going on, either. But we'll never know now, anyway." He looked at her hands, glad to see the redness was fading. "The important thing at this point is to figure out who's breaking into your house and why."

Her shoulders slumped as if the weight of the world was bearing down on them. He longed to pull her close, to reassure her that everything would be fine. But he didn't dare cross the tentative friendship they'd built.

"You're right," she murmured. "I wish I knew what they were looking for."

"I'd like your permission to look around," he said slowly, gazing down at her bowed head. "I'd like to go through Jeremy's things."

Her head snapped up. "Why? Jeremy was not involved in this!"

He took a step back, raising his hand to calm her down. "Please, Kayla, I'm not saying he was involved. But he might have inadvertently stumbled upon the truth. All I'm asking is for you to allow me to poke around."

"No." Kayla's stark refusal caught him off guard. "I'm sorry, Rafe, but I refuse to have Jeremy's good name and reputation tainted by association. If you want to prove Bill Schroeder's guilt, fine. But don't ruin Jeremy's name in order to do it."

He could only gape at her as she spun on her heel and left, shutting the door leading to her room with an irrefutable click.

Kayla couldn't sleep. There was no point to even try. She curled up in her reading chair, wrapped in one of her homemade quilts, trying to grapple with what Rafe had told her.

Bill Schroeder had used his charter fishing boats to smuggle criminals out of the country. And even more frightening was the realization that Bill had likely been murdered.

Jeremy hadn't been involved. No matter what nefarious crimes Bill Schroeder had gotten himself into, she refused to believe her husband had anything remotely to do with it. But she couldn't help but wonder if Rafe might be right. Was it possible Jeremy had stumbled upon something in those last few weeks before his death? Was someone trying to get inside her house because they want to find something Jeremy had?

She frowned because that theory didn't make sense. Why would they wait all this time? Jeremy had been gone for two years. Why bother breaking in now?

Because Bill Schroeder had been here recently? Maybe. She couldn't imagine there was any other reason. It wasn't like her bed-and-breakfast was high-profile.

Suddenly she straightened in her chair, her heart pounding. What about that interview she'd done for the newspaper? The photograph of her and Jeremy together in front of the charter fishing boat had been clearly visible in the snapshot they'd used for the article. Could someone had seen that picture and assumed there were others? Could they be looking for more photographs?

She put a hand over her racing heart. She needed to stop letting her imagination run away with her. Rafe's theories could be wrong. The break-ins might have nothing to do with Schroeder's death.

Although as much as she wanted to believe that, she really couldn't.

An hour later, she ventured back into the kitchen,

beginning to prepare for breakfast. Rafe was a paying guest and he deserved the same treatment as all her other patrons, which meant she needed to bake a batch of her infamous raspberry pastries. She'd wanted to get them finished before Brianna returned from her sleepover.

Brianna. Her fingers stilled in the mound of dough.

Grimly, she realized she had no choice but to let Rafe go through Jeremy's things, whether she liked it or not. She and Brianna wouldn't be safe, not until they knew what the intruder was looking for.

She attacked the dough with a vengeance. So she'd let Rafe go through Jeremy's things, and anything else he wanted to go through as well.

But not without her. She'd help. That way, she'd know if Rafe found anything that would even remotely incriminate Jeremy.

She deserved at least that much, didn't she?

Rafe's phone woke him from a sound sleep. "Yeah?" he muttered.

"DeSilva?" He wasn't thrilled to hear his partner Evan's voice on the line. "You need to get down to the point, pronto. Charlie Turkow has returned."

"Oh yeah?" Rafe stifled a yawn and forced himself awake. "And how would you know? I thought Luke told you to keep an eye on Karl Yancy?"

"There was nothing happening there so I headed over to see if Turkow returned. Do you want me to interview him for you?" Evan's voice was eager.

"No, I'll do it." Rafe tried to mask his irritation. Evan was young and too cocky for his own good. The guy needed to learn how to follow orders.

It was times like this that he missed his former partner, Ben Morrison. Ben deserved to retire, after serving in the coast guard for thirty years, but Rafe still missed him. Rafe hadn't been thrilled to be saddled with the young recruit. Evan wanted lots of action and didn't much care for the tedious parts of the job. "Get back over to keep an eye on Yancy, if he moves and you're not there to tail him, Sanders will not be happy."

"Yeah, yeah, I'm going." Evan hung up and Rafe let out a sigh as he snapped his phone shut.

He quickly dressed and headed downstairs to the kitchen, his stomach rumbling loud enough to wake the dead. The few hours of sleep he'd caught had been better than nothing, but another cup of Kayla's coffee would certainly help clear the remaining cobwebs from his brain.

Ellen and Brianna were seated at the large oak picnic table in the kitchen when he entered the room. He sniffed the air appreciatively. "Something smells wonderful," he said by way of greeting.

"Good morning, Rafe. You're in for a treat, Kayla made her raspberry pastries," Ellen informed him. "The raspberries are from her garden. She freezes them to use throughout the year."

"Hi, Mr. Rafe," Brianna chimed in.

"Hello, *mi nina,*" he said, ruffling her hair as he walked past.

"Have a seat," Kayla said, and he was surprised when she flashed him a smile. Had she already forgiven him that easily? He could only hope.

"Thank you," he murmured. When she put two pastries on a plate for him, along with a steaming bowl of oatmeal, he was impressed with her cooking abilities all over again. He bent his head and silently thanked God for the food before taking a healthy bite of the raspberry pastry. "Delicious."

Kayla blushed a bit and turned back to the stove. He made small talk with Brianna and Ellen as he ate but as soon as he was finished, he stood to leave. "I need to run a few errands, Kayla. Will you please set the security alarm until I get back?"

She looked startled, but nodded. "Sure. How long will you be gone?"

If he had his way, he wouldn't leave at all, but he did have a job to do. His commanding officer expected him to interview Charlie Turkow. Once he did that, he hoped to convince Luke to let him stay here for the next few days. After the second break-in attempt, he was even more convinced he needed to go through Jeremy's things. If Kayla would let him.

"I shouldn't be gone longer than a couple of hours," he told her. "But I really need you to stay inside while I'm gone." The last thing he wanted was for the intruder to return, catching Brianna, Ellen and Kayla home alone.

"We'll stay inside. We have to finish putting up the Christmas decorations, don't we?" Kayla glanced at Ellen and Brianna for confirmation.

"Yay!" Brianna exclaimed.

"That was the plan," Ellen agreed.

Great. More decorations. How many more did Kayla need? He tried not to grimace, knowing he'd put up with the festive atmosphere if it meant the women would stay inside with the security system on. "Sounds good."

Leaving Kayla and Brianna was harder than he'd imagined. He waited until Kayla had engaged the security system, and even then had to force himself to walk out to his jeep, when every cell in his body protested. He sped down the highway toward Pelican Point, trying to reassure himself they'd be fine with the security system engaged.

Thirty-eight minutes later, he reached his destination. Normally the distance was a good forty-five-minute drive. If he kept up like this, he'd end up with a speeding ticket in no time.

He searched the lakeshore for Charlie. Sure enough, Charlie's boat, distinctive with the large bold letters of *Charlie's Charter* along the side, was docked at the pier.

He parked his jeep and tried to think of the best way to approach the grizzled old man. If Bill Schroeder's business had been legitimate, then he would have been a direct competitor of Turkow's. If something shady was going on, he couldn't help but think Charlie knew something about it.

He climbed from his jeep, wondering if he should have worn his dress uniform, instead of casual jeans. Somehow he'd figured that the older man would respond better to less official clothing.

The older man's mostly bald head was covered in a dark knit cap. He popped up from below deck the moment Rafe's foot hit the pier.

"Charlie Turkow?" Rafe said, flashing a casual smile.

"Who wants to know?" Charlie asked ungraciously.

"My name is Rafe DeSilva. I wanted to talk to you for a few minutes, if you don't mind."

The older man's eyes narrowed. "I'm busy."

"I understand, sir, but this won't take long. I was wondering if you'd seen Bill Schroeder lately? Seems he's been missing." Rafe figured since Charlie was out on the water, he probably hadn't heard the news.

"No." Charlie Turkow turned his back, indicating the interview was over.

Rafe figured he needed to get Turkow's attention. "Bill Schroeder is dead. Murdered. Do you know who killed him?"

Charlie's head swiveled around, surprise clearly reflected in his blue eyes. "No. Who did you say you were again?"

"Rafe DeSilva. I'm with the ninth district coast guard. We're investigating Schroeder's death."

"The coast guard?" Charlie's expression went from mild disdain into a frank sneer. "Forget it. I have nothing to say to any Coasties. Do you hear me? Nothing!"

FIVE

Rafe stared after Charlie Turkow when the guy disappeared in the lower cabin of his boat. What was up with the old man? Most of the fishermen had some respect for the coast guard—after all, they were there if the weather changed or if someone needed help because of an engine breakdown. He'd personally helped perform many search and rescue missions for stranded boaters, most of them successful.

Kayla's husband was one of the rare exceptions.

Mulling over this recent turn of events, he walked back toward his jeep. Why would Charlie carry a grudge against the coast guard? Because he was involved in the criminal smuggling activities? Or because he knew something about what was going on and was irritated that the coast guard hadn't been able to stop it?

But then, if Turkow did know something about the criminal smuggling ring, why wouldn't he cooperate with the coast guard? Why shut them out and refuse to talk at all?

When he reached his car, he gave Luke a call. "I didn't get very far with Turkow. He wouldn't talk to me," he said to his commanding officer. "But I don't think he knew about Schroeder's death. The surprise in his eyes when I sprung the news was real."

"So why wouldn't he talk?" Luke demanded.

Rafe blew out a breath. "Apparently he doesn't think very highly of the coast guard. I'm not sure why. Seems odd."

"Do you think he's guilty?"

"Maybe. Given the way he turned on me the minute I mentioned I was with the guard is suspicious enough. I realize some of his lengthy boat trips were to visit his daughter in Michigan, but that could also be a convenient cover, too. I don't think we can take him off our suspect list. The guy is definitely acting strange."

"Hrmph." Luke didn't sound happy. "Dig into Charlie's background. Maybe he had a bad experience with us in the past. If he's innocent, there has to be a reason for his hostility toward us."

"Will do." Rafe hesitated and then asked, "Any word on Karl Yancy?"

"No. Apparently the guy has been holed up in his yacht for a while now. Evan's bored."

Yeah, no kidding. But Rafe didn't say anything against his partner. Their boss expected them to work together and that's exactly what he'd do. "I'm sure if he's part of this, Yancy will move soon. The weather has been cooperating, the temperatures are warmer than usual this time of year. I think the smugglers will make the most of the mild weather while it lasts."

"Let's hope so. With Schroeder dead, we don't have many leads."

"I know. Schroeder's murder only tells us the criminals are fighting amongst themselves. Someone killed him because they wanted a bigger piece of the pie."

"Looks that way," Luke affirmed. "Greed always wins out over loyalty between crooks."

That much was true. "There was another break in attempt at Kayla's B and B. I took off after the intruder, but the guy wore night vision goggles and had a car waiting for him so he got away." Rafe was still annoyed with himself about losing the suspect. "I'm more convinced than ever that there's something inside Kayla's house that is linked to our case."

"Then find it. And fast," Luke advised.

"I will. And I'll check in when I have something to report." He snapped his phone shut and stared out the window for a minute. Since his interview with Charlie had ended before it had even started, he decided to pay his partner a visit. Charlie's hostile attitude bothered him. He really hoped Evan hadn't ignored his request and had approached Charlie before Rafe had arrived. If he found out Evan had in fact messed up his interview, then he'd have no choice but to report Evan to Luke, even though he loathed the idea of ratting out his partner.

He glanced at the clock on the dashboard, figuring there was plenty of time to spare before he'd need to head back to the bed-and-breakfast.

Kayla hadn't seemed angry with him this morning, so he hoped that was a good sign that she'd changed her mind about allowing him to search through her husband's things.

He really needed her cooperation in order to jumpstart their stalled investigation.

Although if he were truly honest with himself, he'd admit that he liked being close to Kayla for reasons that had absolutely nothing to do with his case.

Kayla pulled out the last box of Christmas decorations from the basement. Finally, they were almost finished. She was only going through all of this for Brianna's sake. As well as for her mother-in-law's. She knew Ellen missed Jeremy, too, and the anniversary of his death, so close to Christmas was a difficult reminder for all of them.

Given a choice, Kayla would have preferred to simply pull the covers over her head and hibernate until Christmas was over. But that was hardly fair to Brianna.

"More houses for the Christmas village?" Brianna asked excitedly when Kayla hauled the box up to the main level.

"The last of them," Kayla said with a sigh. Brianna loved setting up the various houses, businesses and figurines for the Christmas village. Kayla had started the collection and in the early years of their marriage, Jeremy had always surprised her with a new piece.

She hadn't added anything new in the two years since he'd died.

"So why exactly is Rafe staying here?" Ellen asked, when Brianna was preoccupied with rearranging her village. "I get the feeling he's interested in you on a personal level."

"No, we're just friends," Kayla said, glancing over at her daughter who was immersed in her project and not listening to the adults. "Brianna looks up to him, though, and I admit her hero worship of Rafe worries me. She's at such a vulnerable age right now, and has been preoccupied with the fact that she doesn't have a father like the other kids at school."

"So why aren't you interested in Rafe?" Ellen's tone was deceptively casual. Kayla glanced at her in surprise. Was her mother-in-law insecure about her place in Kayla and Brianna's future?

"His job means being gone a lot," she said, trying to reassure Ellen. "I had enough of that with Jeremy."

"Jeremy was a good husband and father," Ellen said, jumping to her son's defense. "He took care of his family."

"Yes, he did. When he was home. But those long trips away were hard on me. Remember when Brianna got so sick with her asthma? We were in the emergency department for hours and Jeremy didn't even know." Kayla understood this was a touchy subject for Ellen. "I loved Jeremy, but I was really looking forward to him being home more."

"I know you were," Ellen said, looking contrite. "I thought maybe you weren't interested in Rafe because of his religious beliefs. I admit I was surprised when he prayed before breakfast."

She could have told Ellen that Rafe prayed more than just before meals. They'd already had one conversation regarding his faith and as a result, she'd been curious enough to open the Bible, finding the Book of Psalms that he liked so much. She had to admit, they were comforting to read, not at all what she assumed the Bible would be like. "No, why would his religious beliefs bother me? There aren't many men who would be confident enough to pray in public."

"So you are interested in him." Ellen's expression was a mixture of appalled satisfaction.

Kayla suppressed a sigh. "I told you, we're just friends. Rafe is only staying here because of the break-ins. He's worried about us, that's all."

"Worried because he cares for you, Kayla. You can keep lying to yourself, but I can tell by the way he looks at you." When Kayla opened her mouth to argue, Ellen hurried on, "I can't believe I slept through the excitement last night. You should have woken me up. Does Rafe have any idea why this guy keeps trying to break-in?"

Kayla dropped the subject of Rafe's feelings for her, knowing she had to tread lightly on the subject of Rafe's investigation. Ellen would be even more upset than she'd been, if she discovered how Rafe suspected Jeremy's partner of being a criminal. "Rafe has a lot of theories, but no proof. He's going to search through the house when he gets back." She tried to make light of Rafe's plans. "Who knows, maybe I have some sort of priceless treasure that I don't even know I have."

Ellen seemed to accept her flimsy explanation and changed the subject to fill in Kayla on the latest regarding her sister's broken hip. It sounded as if Irene would be released in a few more days and Ellen was already planning her trip to Arizona to stay with her. Kayla listened with half an ear, her mind whirling. Was Ellen imagining things? Rafe didn't really look at her as if he were interested in a personal relationship. Did he?

And why did the mere possibility make her heart race?

She took several deep breaths to get her emotions under control. Rafe was only a friend. No matter how she responded to him, she needed to keep her feelings grounded in reality. She didn't dare allow herself to care about him as anything more than a friend. What if something happened and their relationship ended? Brianna would be terribly hurt. Her daughter had already lost one father, Kayla couldn't stand the thought of her losing another.

No, she simply couldn't risk it.

She busied herself with making plans for dinner that evening, planning a nice hearty beef stew. But being grounded in reality didn't prevent her from keeping a watchful eye on the clock, wondering when Rafe would return.

So where was Evan? His partner wasn't at the abandoned boathouse where they set up their surveillance of Pelican Point. The boathouse afforded them the ability to closely monitor the lakefront activities. Since Karl Yancy's yacht was still docked at shore, he figured Evan must have taken off again, so Rafe drove all the way back to the coast guard home port substation, and then to Evan's small apartment. He didn't find his partner at either place.

And of course, he wasn't answering his cell phone. Rafe tried several times, before hanging up in irritation. He climbed back into his jeep and went back to Pelican Point, just in time to see Yancy's yacht gliding through the water, heading due north.

After days of sitting around and doing nothing, Yancy was finally on the move.

Rafe ground his teeth together in pent-up frustration as he pulled out a pair of high-powered binoculars and swept his gaze over the area. What was his partner thinking? Evan should be following Yancy right now!

Thinking he'd have to head back to get a craft to follow Yancy himself, he suddenly spotted a small boat way out in the distance in the middle of the lake. He magnified the lenses even more and relaxed a bit when he identified the boat as one of theirs.

Evan was out there, after all. He must have gotten sick of sitting around in the boathouse and had decided to take the cutter out on the water in hopes that Yancy would take the boat out.

Evan got lucky. This time.

Rafe pulled the binoculars away from his eyes and drew out his phone. So if his partner was out on the water, why hadn't Evan answered his phone calls? Because he'd been annoyed to have Rafe checking up on him?

Maybe, but too bad. Evan was young and new to the area. He'd eventually realize that not all investigative operations were a flurry of constant activity. Patience was a virtue.

He put the binoculars away, and called Evan one last time, leaving a terse message: "Call me when Yancy reaches his destination." What he really wanted was for Evan to call so that he could find out if his partner had spoken to Charlie Turkow before Rafe had gotten there.

Rafe climbed back into his jeep. He headed to the highway, taking the shortest and fastest route back to Kayla's.

When he pulled up to the house, darkness had already fallen and the lights of the Christmas tree glowed brightly through the large picture window. The welcoming sight stopped him cold.

Angela would have loved this house. And his unborn child would have loved to play in the woods, too, happily chasing the dog. But his family was gone. Forever. They were in a much better place, but he still missed them.

A different family waited inside, but he couldn't allow himself to get too close.

Swallowing hard, he momentarily closed his eyes and prayed.

Lord, I want to follow the path You've chosen for me. Please give me the strength to protect Kayla and Brianna. Give me the knowledge and wisdom to do right by them. Amen.

Feeling calmer, Rafe climbed out of his jeep and walked up to the front door. He knocked, and instantly Clyde started barking. He waited for Kayla to disarm the security system before opening the door.

"Hi, Rafe," she greeted him, her smile slightly strained. The dog jumped on his legs, seeking attention. He gave Clyde an absent pat on the head. "We were getting worried about you."

"I'm sorry," he murmured, coming inside and closing the door behind him. He watched Kayla activate the alarm, glad she was taking her and her family's safety so seriously. "Everything all right here?"

"Sure. It's been quiet. No problems." She headed back toward the kitchen. "Dinner will be ready in an hour."

He followed her, trying to gauge her mood. "You don't have to cook for me," he protested softly.

She glanced up in surprise. "Why not? I have to cook for myself, Brianna and Ellen so it's no hardship to make more plate for you. It's nothing fancy, just beef stew."

"Beef stew sounds like heaven to me," he told her. "I'm not used to home-cooked meals." Usually he ate on the go at whichever fast-food joint struck him as palatable at the time. "Have you considered my request to go through your husband's things?" he asked hesitantly.

She nodded as she picked up the spoon and stirred the stew. "Yes. I'll allow you to search through Jeremy's things if you let me help. I want to be there if you find something. Since it's so late, I thought we'd wait until after dinner."

"That would be great, Kayla. Thank you." He might have preferred to keep Kayla out of it, but he understood her need to be involved. "Anything I can do to help?"

"No, I'm just waiting for the bread to finish baking."

"Smells delicious." Angela wasn't much for baking the way Kayla seemed to be.

"Mr. Rafe!" Brianna bounded into the room. "Come see our village. Please?"

"Ah, sure." He glanced helplessly at Kayla before allowing Brianna to draw him into the great room. Beneath the tree, she'd created an entire tiny village, complete with movie theater, bookstore, ski chalet and an ice-skating rink. There were tiny figurines and cars set in various locations, too. "Wow, Brianna. This is amazing."

"I know. My mom's been collecting them since she was a girl," Brianna announced. "But she told me I'll get it one day."

"That's nice." Telling himself not to get too close to Kayla and Brianna was one thing, actually keeping his distance was another. Everywhere he looked were reminders of home and family. The pine scent surrounding the tree brought back memories of his and Angela's first Christmas together.

Blocking out the past wasn't easy. He made a fire in the fireplace as Brianna chatted about their day and then made an excuse to escape to his room, using the time to begin his search on Charlie Turkow and potential links to the coast guard.

Kayla called him down to dinner less than an hour later. He bowed his head to pray, noticing that everyone else waited for him to finish before starting to eat. Next time, he'd ask them to join him in prayer.

The beef stew and the homemade bread were delicious, but he didn't linger over the meal, anxious to finish so they could begin their search.

Kayla cleared the table, and he jumped up to help,

figuring two could get the job done faster than one. Ellen took over, shooing them out of the way.

"I'll do the dishes. Brianna can help."

"Aw, Grandma," Brianna whined. "I don't wanna help."

"Why not? I thought you liked helping your grandma?" For a moment Ellen looked hurt by Brianna's refusal.

"I do," Brianna agreed. "I'll help." Then she brightened. "Can we go Christmas shopping tomorrow?"

"Sure."

Rafe went into the great room, waiting for Kayla to join him.

"Where would you like to start?" she asked.

"Does Jeremy have anything here related to the charter fishing business?" he asked, hoping Kayla hadn't tossed anything out.

"There are a couple of boxes in the attic, I think," she said. "But I don't know if they'll be much help."

"It's worth a try." Rafe hung back, letting her walk up the stairs leading to the second floor. "Where is the access to the attic?"

"Actually, it's hidden in the closet of your guest room," Kayla said heading for the doorway leading into his room.

"My room?" Surprised, he followed her in, glad that years of living on a boat meant that he kept his things neatly tucked away. The fact that the attic access happened to be in the room where the break-ins were focused only reaffirmed his suspicions. "Was this the same room Greg Landrum used?"

"No, he was two rooms over," Kayla said, as she opened the closet door and pulled on a thin cord that hung down from the ceiling. A trap door in the ceiling fell open and she unfolded a narrow ladder that was tucked inside. "Brr, it's cold up there. And dark. We'll need a flashlight."

"I have one right here." Always prepared, Rafe had already pulled out the flashlight from the back of his jeep. He flicked it on and put a hand on Kayla's slim shoulder, preventing her from climbing up the ladder. "Would you mind waiting? I'd like to check things out first."

She hesitated and then moved aside. Rafe gingerly stepped on the ladder, testing it to make sure it would hold his weight.

"Jeremy went up there all the time. I'm sure it's fine," Kayla said.

"All right." He climbed the ladder, holding the flashlight in one hand. Kayla was right, the air was much cooler up here.

At the top, he poked his head through the opening and then cast the flashlight around the area. His pulse jumped when he noticed the boxes Kayla mentioned. They stood open, the contents strewn messily around the room.

Someone had already been up there.

SIX

"Do you see them?" Kayla asked, craning her neck and trying to see when Rafe stood silently for several long moments at the top of the attic ladder. "I'm sure I stored the boxes up there."

"Yes, they're here." Rafe's long, lean legs disappeared from view as he climbed the rest of the way up. He leaned over the edge, peering down at her, his expression grave. "Kayla, someone's been up here."

"What?" She quickly ascended the ladder to see for herself. She sucked in a harsh breath when she saw the mess, files, papers and notebooks lying haphazardly on the floor. "I didn't leave it like this," she whispered.

"No, I'm sure you didn't." Rafe's expression in the glow of the flashlight was grim. "But obviously we know what your odd guest Greg Landrum was doing. The two burglary attempts were caught before the intruder made it inside, so this had to be done by someone who'd been here. You mentioned how you heard loud noises from Greg Landrum's room at night. I'm sure you heard him up here while he was searching through your husband's things."

"I don't believe it." Kayla shivered and not from the cold. The very thought of Greg Landrum being up here made her blood run cold. "So, does this mean he already found what he was looking for?"

"I doubt it, since Landrum, or somebody he works for, continues to try to break in." Keeping his head down, Rafe walked over to pick up one file, tucking the scattered papers back inside. "No, the more I think about it, the more I'm convinced they didn't find what they wanted."

"Maybe because it's not up here." Kayla rubbed her hands on her arms, hating the feeling of being violated. She'd known Greg Landrum was an odd man, but she really hadn't considered he'd been searching through her attic while he was a guest in her home. Not a nice way to return her hospitality.

"Do you have anything of Jeremy's stored in your private rooms?" Rafe asked, continuing to straighten the mess.

"No." She'd kept their family photographs of course, but she'd given his clothes to charity so that they would be put to good use. "There's one small box containing his sports trophies from high school that I returned to Ellen, but that's about all. Jeremy wasn't big into collecting things. Except when it came to fishing. And all his fishing stuff is mixed in with the business."

Rafe knelt beside the largest box and began poking around inside. She crossed over to another box and did the same. "So what exactly are we looking for?" she asked, noting that most of what was in the box were old bookkeeping records from the charter fishing trips Jeremy had taken. Her husband had kept painstakingly detailed notes, tracking where the best fishing was so he could take other guests to the same spots.

He shrugged. "I don't know. I suspect we'll know once we find it."

"Great. That sure helps. Not." Kayla decided that rather than searching through Jeremy's things, since she doubted she'd know it when she found it, she'd concentrate on cleaning up the mess. She sat down, and began the painstaking job of putting Jeremy's files back the way he'd left them, in chronological order.

Rafe glanced over at her. "You don't need to stay, Kayla," he said in a low voice. "It's cold up here. I promise I'll show you whatever I find."

She looked up in surprise. "I know." Somehow, it felt wrong to leave him alone to poke through Jeremy's things. She didn't exactly relish the trip down memory lane, but couldn't force herself to leave the task to him, either. But her fingers were already turning numb with cold, so she stood and headed back toward the ladder intending to get some gloves. "I'll be back in a few minutes."

"Take your time," he said, as if sensing how difficult this would be for her. She went back downstairs to put on a heavy wool sweater and some knit gloves. Brianna and Ellen were watching *The Grinch Who Stole Christmas* on television, so she left them to their movie, heading back upstairs.

Rafe was looking at the guest logs of Jeremy's trips. He glanced up at her when she returned. "Tell me, did your husband take photographs of his guests with their catch?"

"All the time." She never quite understood the appeal, but had always acted suitably impressed when Jeremy showed her what his clients had caught. "There should be a whole stack of photographs in here somewhere since he always kept a copy for himself, too. He often used them for marketing purposes."

"Help me look for them," Rafe suggested.

Abandoning her plan to put everything back in order, she went through one box while Rafe searched the other. She found lots of notes, some nautical maps, receipts of various expenses but no photographs.

Not a single one.

Disturbed by their absence, she rocked back on her heels. Rafe had come up empty as well. "How odd that the photographs are missing. And there were some other pictures, too, not just of Jeremy's clients. But some of Jeremy and Bill together in front of their boat."

"And you're sure the photographs were up here? You didn't store them someplace else?"

She shook her head. "I'm positive."

"What about that framed photograph of you and Jeremy hanging down in your kitchen? Was that taken about the same time as these others?"

She frowned. "Yes, I guess so. I think that photograph was taken on their one-year anniversary of being in business. I was pregnant with Brianna at the time."

Rafe blew out an exasperated breath as he glanced at the boxes. "So Greg Landrum must have taken the photographs."

"I have to assume so. But why?" She didn't understand. "What good are a bunch of old photographs? What do they prove?"

"I'm not sure," Rafe murmured. "But I think whatever Landrum found in the pictures must not have been exactly what he was looking for. There must be something else here. Something they still want." The grim expression in his eyes caused an icy fear to seep into her bones, and not from the chilly attic temperature.

Rafe couldn't sleep. Long after Kayla had returned downstairs to go to bed, Rafe stayed awake. After checking his cell phone several times, looking for a missed call from his partner, he tossed the instrument aside with disgust and reached for his laptop.

Evan hadn't called. Because his quarry hadn't reached his destination? Somehow, Rafe doubted it. Surely by this time, Karl Yancy had docked somewhere. No one drove a boat all night without taking a rest. He'd give Evan until the morning to touch base, and if his partner didn't call him by then, he'd go to Luke Sanders.

But his partner's lack of communication wasn't the real reason he couldn't sleep. The knowledge of how Greg Landrum had been inside Kayla's house gnawed at him.

There was a possibility that Landrum had killed Bill Schroeder. What if Landrum had intended to harm Kayla or Brianna, too? Greg Landrum could very easily have left them both dead. The realization sent a shaft of fear straight through his heart.

Landrum had gotten way too close. Rafe wanted Kayla far away from this guy since they had no idea what he was really capable of. Sure, the burglary attempts hadn't involved hurting anyone. But what if that changed?

Rafe continued searching the Internet, looking at anything connected to Landrum. He needed a photograph. Using his secure access to the coast guard's search engines, he eventually hit pay dirt.

The Department of Motor Vehicle Registration for the state of Illinois gave him exactly what he needed. A grainy photograph of Greg Landrum and the man looking back at him didn't resemble the guy Kayla had described. She'd estimated her guest as being in his mid-thirties with dishwater blond hair. The statistics on the man he'd found claimed he was forty-seven years old, his hair brown and his eyes hazel. He was also listed as being six-feet tall, and two hundred and fifty pounds. Kayla hadn't given him a height and a weight estimate, but she'd given him the impression that the guy who'd stayed here had been much smaller than that.

He saved the photograph to his hard drive. Kayla would need to verify the Greg Landrum he'd found in Chicago wasn't the same man who'd stayed as a guest. And once she did, then what? Was it possible Landrum had given her a fake address?

Landrum wasn't a common last name. He broadened his search, to make sure he didn't miss any other potential hits for Kayla's mysterious guest. Other than a sixty-nine-year-old gerontologist, who he ruled out easily enough, he didn't find any.

He smiled grimly. The idiot would have been smarter to use a bogus name like Greg Jones. Now he knew the odd guest had used a fake ID. For the first time since learning about Schroeder's death, he felt a sense of excitement. Landrum had made one mistake. Two, if you counted how he'd interrupted the second break-in attempt.

All Rafe had to do was to figure out how to capitalize on them.

He shut his laptop down and turned off the lights. If he didn't get some sleep, then he wouldn't be able to protect Kayla.

One thing was for certain. He wouldn't allow Kayla to rent out any more rooms to strangers. Not until he'd caught the man who kept trying to break in.

And not until they'd found Schroeder's murderer.

He closed his eyes and prayed. *Please help give me the wisdom to keep Kayla and Brianna safe, Lord.*

* * *

Kayla prepared another batch of breakfast pastries, peach-filled this time. She couldn't deny that she liked having Rafe here to cook for. Something about having a man around was oddly reassuring. Clyde sat at her feet, his ever-hopeful gaze waiting for a scrap to fall so he could pounce on it.

She stepped around the dog as she worked. She'd slept through the night, feeling safe between Rafe sleeping upstairs and having set her security system. Somehow, she'd doubted the intruder would return, now that Rafe had taken off after him. He had to know Rafe was waiting.

When Rafe came down to the kitchen carrying a notebook computer, he looked a little rough around the edges, as if he could have used more sleep. Wordlessly, she poured him a cup of coffee.

"Thanks," he murmured, setting down the computer so he could take a sip. He opened the laptop, turning it so the screen faced her way. "Do you recognize this guy?" he asked.

"No." She glanced at him curiously. "Never saw him before in my life. Why?"

"Because this is Greg Landrum from Chicago." Rafe closed the laptop cover. "I haven't found any other potential Greg Landrums in the Midwest, either. I believe your guy used an assumed name."

Her coffee curdled in her stomach. "That's scary. He gave me a credit card number, but he also paid in cash." Hearing the murmur of voices from Ellen and Brianna, she glanced toward the doorway of her private suite of rooms. "Don't mention this to Ellen, please? I don't want her to worry."

"All right," Rafe nodded. "But Kayla, you can't keep

renting rooms out to strangers. Not until we get to the bottom of this."

She wanted to protest, but knew Rafe was right. Hadn't she already made that decision last night, after seeing the mess in the attic? She couldn't believe Greg Landrum had searched her home. Still, her business was already suffering. It wouldn't be easy to turn down any last-minute calls for a room. She grimaced. "Well, lucky for you, I don't have any guests booked until the middle of January."

"I'm sorry, Kayla." Rafe's dark eyes reflected his regret. "But it's for the best."

"I know." She tried to smile. "Breakfast is almost ready."

"I need another favor," Rafe said slowly. "Do you think you could describe your mystery guest to a police artist?"

She lifted a brow in surprise. "I don't know. Maybe."

"I'd like you to try." Rafe leaned forward, earnestly. "At the moment, I don't have anything else to go on. A picture of this guy would be a place to start."

The thought of working with a police artist was a little intimidating, but she couldn't refuse Rafe's request. After all, wouldn't helping Rafe help her, too? The quicker they found the guy, the less likely she'd have to turn down a paying guest. "All right. But I've never done something like this before. I don't know if the drawing will be accurate."

"You'd be surprised. Thank you, Kayla. I'll make the arrangements." Rafe's voice rang with satisfaction. "This will work. You'll see."

She wished she could be as positive. She set the tray of peach pastries on the table. When Ellen came in a few minutes later, she glanced at her mother-in-law. "Where's Brianna?"

"Brushing her teeth."

Kayla poured her mother-in-law some coffee. "Would you mind keeping an eye on Brianna for a few hours today? Rafe and I have an errand to run."

Ellen's eyes widened with frank curiosity as she glanced between Rafe and Kayla. "Ah, sure. Brianna and I were going to do some Christmas shopping this afternoon anyway."

"I don't know if that's a good idea," Rafe spoke up. "Couldn't you just hang around here with the security system engaged?"

"What would we do here all day?" Ellen wanted to know. She swung back to face Kayla. "Are we in danger?"

The burglar attempts had been very real, but so far, there hadn't been any threat to anyone on a personal level. "Rafe?" Feeling helpless, she glanced at him. "What do you think? Would Christmas shopping be the worst thing in the world? The mall will be crowded, considering there is less than ten days left before Christmas."

He sighed, swiped a hand down his face, looking like he wanted to refuse, but then nodded. "You're probably right. Christmas shopping in broad daylight should be fine. I would ask one favor, though. We all need to leave at the same time, so I can set the security system. Ellen, you and Brianna have to stay shopping until we've returned. That way, I can go through the house first, just to make sure everything is fine."

"Sounds reasonable," Ellen admitted.

"Thanks, Rafe," Kayla murmured.

Brianna skipped into the room. "Hi, Mommy. Hi,

Grandma. Hi, Mr. Rafe. I'm hungry," she announced, climbing up to sit at the table. Kayla took a seat next to her daughter.

Ellen sat across from them, and there was an awkward moment as they all glanced at Rafe, unwilling to begin eating until he'd finished his before-meal prayer.

"I'll say grace," he murmured, bowing his head. "Heavenly Father, thank You for the food You have provided here for us this morning. We are blessed to have You watching over us. Please keep us safe as we begin our day. Amen."

There was a silent pause, until Brianna said, "Amen."

Kayla glanced at her daughter in surprise. They hadn't prayed much when Jeremy was alive. A prayer before bedtime at the most.

She watched as Rafe helped himself to a peach pastry. When he caught her gaze, he smiled. Her stomach clenched, and she went hot all over, feeling the effects of his smile all the way down to her knees. Flustered, she turned her attention to her daughter, although what Brianna chatted about, she had no idea.

Her attention was still riveted on Rafe.

He was strong and gentle, handsome and yet so very spiritual. She'd never met a man like Rafe before.

Keeping her distance from him while he was a guest in her home was proving to be more difficult than she'd ever imagined.

Rafe was thrilled with how easily Brianna had participated in his prayer. This must be the path God had chosen for him. He would absolutely help Kayla find her way to the Lord. Despite his lack of sleep, his mood was upbeat as he drove Kayla back to the police station in Green Bay, twenty miles north of Pelican Point.

Now that it was just the two of them in the car, he was at a loss for words. He couldn't seem to find the friendly atmosphere they'd shared before.

Because she was more than just a friend?

"There really isn't any danger, is there?" she asked, suddenly breaking the silence.

His chest tightened at the fear laced in her tone. "I probably overreacted back there," he admitted. "Greg Landrum had already been a guest in your home. He didn't use the opportunity to hurt you or Brianna. I just can't completely relax until we find the guy."

"And you really think the police sketch will help?"

"I do." He'd already planned to approach Charlie Turkow again, flashing the picture and watching the older man's reaction. "We can alert all the coast guard cutters to be on the lookout for him."

"What if he's not out on the water?" she asked, perplexed.

He couldn't believe the guy wasn't involved in his case. "I think he has to be linked to the criminal smuggling ring and to Schroeder's death."

She paled. "What if he killed Bill?"

"It's possible." And that was the main reason he'd overreacted. "But Landrum, or whatever this guy's real name is, isn't the only one involved. Someone is helping him. That's why I really need you to do this sketch."

"I understand." Kayla didn't ask anything more and when they arrived at the police station, she went right to work, taking her role in creating a viable sketch seriously.

Rafe didn't watch the artist work, preferring to wait for the finished product, but he sat back, observing how Kayla interacted with the police artist, Christine Andrews.

"No, his face is a little more round," Kayla said, her forehead scrunched with concentration. "And his eyes were closer together. Beady. Yes, like that."

"What about his chin?" Christine asked. "Pointy? Round? Cleft?"

"Weak." Kayla shrugged helplessly when Christine raised her brows. "I don't know how else to describe it. He had a weak chin. Rounded I guess, but not very prominent."

Christine's pencil scratched against the paper as she drew and then erased and drew some more. He couldn't tear his gaze from Kayla. She was so beautiful, not like a model or movie-star, but in a girl-next-door kind of way.

What if he'd met Kayla before Angela? Would he have still married Angela?

Stupid question. Immediately he felt ashamed for even thinking such a thing. Of course he would have. He'd loved Angela. Had loved his wife with his whole heart and soul. Had wanted to die when he'd lost both his wife and baby.

A boy. The son he'd never have.

No, as much as he admired Kayla and adored Brianna, they couldn't take Angela's and his son's place in his heart. Never. He and Kayla were just friends.

Friends.

Nothing more.

"No, there's something wrong," Kayla fretted. "It's not right. Something's wrong."

Christine never lost her patience. "Okay, let's rule out what could be wrong. The forehead? The nose? His eyes?"

"No, his eyes are right." Kayla stared hard at the sketch. "Maybe it's his cheeks. They were more prominent. Gaunt maybe, in spite of his round face. I kept thinking he needed to eat more."

"Okay, how about this?" Christine took her eraser to a portion of the picture and then tried again. After a few minutes she turned the sketch toward Kayla.

"Yes." Kayla's tone held satisfaction. "That's him. That's the man who rented a room from me."

"Let me see," Rafe commanded, leaning forward urgently. Christine obliged by turning the sketch, but his heart sank with sharp disappointment when he studied the man's face.

He didn't recognize the guy.

SEVEN

"Do you know him?" Kayla asked.

"No, I'm afraid not." Rafe had hoped that the sketch would jog his memory. That he'd instantly remember the guy meeting at the lakefront with Bill Schroeder in the months they'd watched him.

No such luck.

Truth be told, the guy didn't look very threatening. Kayla described him as gaunt and Rafe had to agree. And aside from his beady eyes, the man in the sketch could be your average John Doe. There was nothing at all that indicated the guy was dangerous. He frowned and gave himself a mental shake. Physical appearances meant nothing. There was still a strong possibility this guy had murdered Bill Schroeder.

"You did a great job, Kayla," he said, reassuring her when he noticed her expression appeared anxious. "The sketch is perfect."

She relaxed, giving him a small smile. "I'm glad I could help."

"You helped a lot." Rafe rose to his feet and took the sketch from Christine's outstretched hand. "Thanks, Christine. I appreciate your assistance with this."

"Anytime," she said, lifting her shoulder in a graceful shrug. "Take care, Rafe."

"Will do." Taking Kayla's arm, he escorted her from the police station.

"So now what?" she asked, as they climbed back into his jeep.

He glanced at the clock on his dashboard, a little surprised to realize Kayla had completed her sketch in less than an hour. With any luck, Ellen and Brianna wouldn't be shopped out for a while yet. "Do you mind if we stop at the coast guard substation? I'd like to get this picture in the hands of the rest of the men as soon as possible."

"No, of course I don't mind." Kayla relaxed against the seat cushion. "I'm glad that's over, although it wasn't as bad as I expected."

He chuckled. "I don't know, for a while there you were getting frustrated."

"True." She laughed and the sound wrapped itself around his heart. He tried to ignore the sensation. He was here to protect Kayla and Brianna from harm, and to help her find the path to the Lord. Nothing else.

So why did his thoughts keep heading down a dangerous, more personal path? He turned up the Christmas music on the radio in an attempt to drown out his thoughts.

Unfortunately, the Christmas music only made him think about Angela. And their unborn son. And how his lack of planning had failed them both. He scowled, tempted to change the station, but suspected that seeing as there was only a week until Christmas, it was likely the other stations were also playing Christmas tunes.

Several long minutes passed before Kayla spoke

again. "You really think it's possible this man killed Bill Schroeder?" she asked, staring at the sketch.

"Yeah. I do." Keep focused on business, he reminded himself. Distractions would only put Kayla in harm's way. "If not him personally, then someone he works for. Either way, he's the best lead we have at the moment."

"Poor Bill," Kayla murmured. "I should really give Jeanine a call. I know she divorced Bill, but this still must be a horrible shock."

"They didn't have any children?" he asked, even though he knew from his research they didn't have any, he was curious about the guy. Often the motivations behind the crimes were the toughest to figure out.

"They tried, but apparently it wasn't meant to be. Jeanine wanted to adopt, but Bill refused. I think in the end their marriage suffered because of it."

It was a little odd to be thinking of their main suspect as a man who'd tried to have a family. So why had Bill Schroeder become involved in the criminal smuggling ring? Money? Greed? For thrills? What?

At this point, they might never figure out what his real motives were. And truth be told, he was more interested in shutting the operation down than understanding the why behind the crime.

He pulled into the parking lot of the coast guard substation a few minutes later. Taking the sketch from Kayla's hands, he led the way inside. He headed straight to Luke Sanders' office. His commanding officer saw them coming and rose to meet them halfway.

Rafe raised his hand in a sharp salute. "Sir. This is Mrs. Kayla Wilson, owner of Kayla's bed-and-breakfast. Kayla, this is my lieutenant commander, Luke Sanders."

Luke returned Rafe's salute and then accepted Kayla's outstretched hand. "Pleasure to meet you, ma'am."

"Likewise," she murmured shyly.

"Here's a sketch of our suspect," Rafe said, getting straight to the point. He handed the sketch to Luke. "He rented a room at Kayla's B and B under the name of Gregory Landrum, giving a Chicago address. But the real Gregory Landrum from Chicago is at least ten to fifteen years older and heavier by almost a hundred pounds."

"Why would he rent a room under an assumed name?" Luke asked.

"As a cover to search through her husband's business records," Rafe explained. "Mrs. Wilson stored everything from the charter fishing operation in the attic and we discovered someone has been up there, going through them. Everything had been pulled out of the boxes and tossed on the floor. From what we could determine, all the photographs are missing. We believe this man is the one who keeps trying to break in."

His commanding officer's glance cut over to Kayla, as if gauging how much she knew about her husband's business dealings. "The stolen photographs aren't enough?"

"Apparently not, sir. We think it's possible something is still hidden in her home. Or someone thinks there's something still hidden in her home. Either way, we need more time to complete a thorough search."

"Hmm." Luke stared at the sketch for a long moment before meeting Rafe's waiting gaze. "All right, I'll give you the time you need. Keep me informed of your progress."

"Yes, sir." Rafe hesitated, and then asked, "Have you

heard from my partner? Last I knew Evan was following Yancy's yacht."

"Yes, Evan checked in this morning," Luke affirmed. "Said Yancy has his yacht moored near Harbor Springs, Michigan. No movement toward shore yet and no evidence of another passenger. Evan is going to stay on him to see what happens."

Perturbed at the news, Rafe simply nodded. How would Evan know if there was a passenger seeking to escape into Canada when he was way out in the middle of the lake when Yancy took off from shore? If Evan had waited on shore, then he might have gotten a glimpse of a passenger climbing on board.

He debated giving Luke his opinion, but then decided against it. No point in bringing his commanding officer into the personal issue going on between him and his partner. Evan was his junior partner since Rafe had many more years of service under his belt, but Evan obviously had issues with taking leadership advice from Rafe.

And if Karl Yancy did have a criminal passenger on board, Evan would eventually get a glimpse of the guy once they arrived at their final destination. Surely Evan wouldn't mess this up, would he?

"I'd like to make a copy of the sketch," Rafe said, turning back to the issue at hand. "Before you send it out to the rest of the crew."

"Sure."

Rafe made a quick copy and then handed it back. "Anything else, sir?"

"No, that's all for now." Luke nodded toward Kayla. "Nice meeting you, Mrs. Wilson. Take care of yourself."

"I will."

Kayla was unusually quiet on the ride back to her bed-and-breakfast. He glanced at her several times, but she continued to stare out the passenger side window, as if lost in her thoughts.

"Are you all right?" he asked finally, when the silence had stretched beyond his patience.

She looked at him, her expression troubled. "I was thinking about Jeremy."

His fingers tightened on the steering wheel. For some reason, the way Kayla clung to her dead husband got under his skin. "What about him?"

"You said you were only watching Bill Schroeder for the past few months, right?"

"Yes," he said slowly, as the direction of the conversation made him feel as he was treading on thin ice.

"And there's no reason to believe Jeremy was involved in the criminal smuggling?" This was a question more than a statement of fact.

"That's true." Of course they didn't have any reason to believe Jeremy wasn't involved in the criminal activity, either, but he didn't go there.

"So I shouldn't be worried that Jeremy's death could be the result of something more sinister?" Kayla said finally. "Like murder? The way Bill was murdered?"

Kayla held her breath, waiting for Rafe's response. She didn't know why the thought hadn't occurred to her before now. But for some reason, standing in the middle of the coast guard home port substation and meeting Lieutenant Commander Luke Sanders had made Rafe's investigation more real.

More official.

What if Jeremy had stumbled upon the truth? And had died because of it?

"I don't know, Kayla," he said finally. "I wish I could tell you for sure one way or the other, but the honest answer is that I simply don't know."

She couldn't seem to leave it alone. "But the circumstances around Jeremy's death would have been investigated, right? And I'm sure they would have told me if there was some question about how he died."

"Yes, I'm sure they would have," Rafe agreed. "I was part of the team who found his boat and I can tell you, we didn't find anything suspicious. Accidents like drowning are required to be reviewed by the ME."

"You investigated his death?" she echoed in surprise.

He glanced at her, his expression serious. "I was part of the team that searched for him, yes. As I would anyone lost in the water."

She didn't know why she was surprised to hear he'd searched for Jeremy, but she was. Two years ago she hadn't even known Rafe. Now she knew their paths had crossed, even then. She went back to the subject that wouldn't leave her alone. "Do you know for certain how long the criminal smuggling ring has been going on?"

"At least a year, as far as we can tell, maybe longer," Rafe conceded. "But again, there's no way to know exactly when Bill Schroeder became involved. It could have easily been after your husband's death." He glanced at her, compassion warming his gaze. "Don't torture yourself about this, Kayla. You're right. If the ME had thought the circumstances of your husband's death were suspicious, there would have been a more in-depth investigation. Don't borrow trouble. Let's just concentrate on moving forward from here, okay?"

Rafe was right, she knew he was, but it wasn't easy to let go of the nagging thoughts. Dealing with Jeremy's death had been difficult enough, but she couldn't comprehend how she'd feel if she discovered he was murdered. She forced a smile. "I'll try."

"Good. When we get back to your B and B, we need to broaden our search."

"Broaden the search where?" Kayla couldn't imagine what else there was to look through. "Everything of Jeremy's is in the attic."

"Kayla, I need you to think about this carefully. Is there any possibility Bill Schroeder could have hid something without you knowing about it?" he asked. "Any way at all?"

Hid something? In her house? She stared at Rafe, casting her memory back to the day Bill had surprised her by stopping over when she hadn't heard from him in over a year. He'd seemed ill at ease, holding the door open as if unsure of whether or not to come in. He'd finally come in, but before the door closed, Clyde caught sight of a squirrel and took off into the woods. She told Bill to have a seat moments before she and Brianna had immediately gone after the dog. Just a couple of months earlier, they'd let Clyde run loose in the woods and he'd suffered a close encounter with a skunk. The horrible stench still burned in her memory and she'd never wanted to risk that mess again. Hence their frantic search for Clyde.

Thinking back, she didn't think she'd been gone very long but maybe it was just enough time. "Yes, it's possible," she finally admitted.

"Really?" Rafe's intense gaze pierced her.

"The day he came over, the dog got loose. Brianna and I went after Clyde while he waited inside."

"Long enough for him to hide something?" Rafe persisted.

"Yes, about ten to fifteen minutes." She shivered despite the mild temperatures outside. Why would Bill purposefully drag her into this mess? Because he'd been desperate? Or had he believed whatever secret he'd left would be safe with her?

"I'm sorry, Kayla," Rafe said in a low tone, reaching over to take her hand in his. His hand was strong and warm, and for the life of her she couldn't convince herself to let go.

She tried to smile. "It's not your fault, Rafe."

He gave her hand a gentle, reassuring squeeze. "Maybe not, although I still feel responsible. But know this, Kayla. I will keep you and Brianna safe. I promise."

She nodded, her throat tight with repressed fear. Sitting here with her hand engulfed within his, she acknowledged she did trust Rafe to keep them safe. Already couldn't imagine being at the bed-and-breakfast without him.

But what about once the danger had passed? Rafe would go back to his regular coast guard duties, saving the lives of those who worked or played on the water. The thirty-five miles separating their respective homes would seem like thirty-five hundred. Their paths would rarely cross.

He'd be out on the water and she'd go back to fighting to keep her business alive and raising Brianna.

Suddenly, the rather bleak glimpse of her future seemed incredibly lonely and not the least bit appealing.

Kayla waited in the jeep as Rafe deactivated her security system and then went inside to do a search of her house. She could hear Clyde barking as Rafe took the time to let him out on his chain.

She felt a little foolish sitting inside the car when two people searching the interior of the house would go much faster. But Rafe had flat-out refused to allow her to help.

She reminded herself that Rafe knew what he was doing, and that his overly protective nature would only help to keep them safe.

Fifteen minutes later he came back outside. "Doesn't look like anything has been disturbed," he told her as they walked inside.

She automatically flipped on the lights for the Christmas tree, knowing how much Brianna loved them. "Do you mind if I give Ellen a call to let her know it's okay to return?" she asked, reaching for her cell phone. "I think they're probably tired of shopping."

"Sure." He waited until she'd finished talking to her mother-in-law and then asked, "Do you mind if I begin searching your private suite of rooms?"

The thought of Rafe going through her private things was disconcerting, to say the least. But she understood why he felt the need to be thorough. "I guess not, although I'd like to finish cleaning up the mess in the attic first."

"I'll help. Once we get the attic finished up, we can expand our search."

Rafe headed upstairs and she followed, taking Clyde with her even though she expected Ellen and Brianna to return at any moment.

The papers and files scattered around the boxes in the attic weren't as abundant as she remembered. Belatedly, she realized Rafe must have spent some time putting everything away last night after she'd gone to bed.

"I can take care of the rest of this," she said, putting a hand on his arm to stop him from bending down to begin replacing files in the open box. "Why don't you go ahead and start the rest of your search? I'll join you when I'm finished up here."

He went still, glancing at her hand for a brief moment before meeting her gaze. "I'd rather stay close," he murmured. The cool air suddenly warmed between them as he gazed deeply into her eyes.

Suddenly, it was difficult to breathe. And she couldn't tear her gaze away. Rafe wanted to stay with her? Because of the risk of potential danger? Or something more?

She told herself to back away, but as usual, her conscience ignored her command. Rafe's intense midnight eyes held her captive.

"Kayla," he murmured, reaching up to lightly brush a strand of hair from her cheek. She held her breath, sensing the intent in his eyes when he leaned toward her. When his mouth brushed hers, ever so gently, she wanted to throw herself into his arms, never letting go.

Clyde barked loudly from Rafe's room, startling them badly and breaking off the kiss. "What in the world?" Rafe muttered as he headed over to the attic trap door.

She put a hand over her racing heart. The dog had scared her to death, no question about it. "Brianna and Ellen are probably home. I'm sure it's fine."

"That would explain his reaction," Rafe said. Sure enough, the dog quieted down almost instantly. He stared at her for a moment from across the dimly lit space.

An awkward silence fell so she dropped to her knees beside the open box and began straightening files.

Jeremy had been fanatical about keeping his files in precise order. She felt compelled to put them back in the same order he'd left them in. "I'll finish up here," she said again.

Rafe didn't respond right away, but she could feel his gaze watching her. Finally she looked up at him. "What's wrong?"

He opened his mouth as if to say something, but then slowly shook his head. "Nothing's wrong. I just wanted to make sure you weren't upset with me for overstepping my bounds."

She sat back on her haunches. "No, Rafe. I'm not upset with you. Confused, maybe, but not upset."

"Confused is a good word," he murmured, letting out a sigh. "Kayla, I feel like I should apologize, but I can't lie. I'm not sorry I kissed you. But I also can't allow you to distract me from my assignment. I need to keep focused on the investigation. Nothing else can take priority."

"I understand," she said with a nod, hiding the stab of disappointment. What was wrong with her? Why couldn't she seem to keep her distance from Rafe? One kiss and suddenly she welcomed him into her life with open arms? She picked up another of Jeremy's files. "I'm not sure I'm ready to be a distraction," she told him honestly. "I loved Jeremy and I'm afraid to open myself up like that again."

"I feel the same way," he confessed.

"Really?" She remembered he said something about losing someone he'd loved and she realized she didn't know much about Rafe's personal life. He was so handsome, she couldn't believe he didn't have women falling over themselves to be with him. In fact, she hadn't been very nice to him the first time they'd met because she'd assumed with his handsome looks he was a bit of a player. But over these past few days, he didn't act at all as if he were pining away for a more active social life. He didn't even seem to notice the beautiful police artist, Christine. The entire time she'd worked on the sketch, she'd felt his gaze on her, not on Christine.

And just now, he'd kissed her.

"You know I lost Jeremy, but who did you lose, Rafe?" she asked.

He hesitated so long she thought he wasn't going to answer. "My wife and our unborn child," he said finally.

Her eyes widened and the blood drained out of her face. "Your wife?" she repeated in an agonized tone. "And your baby?" She couldn't even imagine. And here she'd thought he was out dating every night, when obviously nothing could have been farther from the truth.

"Yes. A boy. I named him Josué, Joshua in English, and buried him beside my wife."

A son. And his wife. Stunned she could only stare at him. What could she say to that? His pain had to have been all encompassing. Words seemed so inadequate. "I'm so sorry."

"Me, too." He grimaced a bit. "But Kayla, the only thing that kept me going during those dark days and nights after they were gone was my faith. As much as I didn't understand why God had taken them, I also knew I wasn't alone."

She'd never thought of faith as being a solution for feeling alone. The days after Jeremy's death, knowing she had to be strong for Brianna was the only thing that had kept her going.

And if she'd lost Brianna, too? No, she couldn't imagine what would have happened.

Psalm 23 verse 4 came to her mind. *Even though I walk through the valley of the shadow of death, I will fear no evil for you are with me; your rod and your staff, they comfort me.*

She didn't realize she'd said the verse out loud until Rafe came closer. "You've been reading the Bible?" he asked, an awed expression on his face.

She flushed and nodded. "Just the Psalms. I can see why they're your favorite. They're so beautiful, almost like songs. Or poems. They seem to tell a story."

A brilliant smile creased his features. "They are exactly like poems. I'm so glad you like them."

She thought it was so strange in a way to be talking with a man about the Bible. Her brother had turned to God with her sister-in-law's help, but that was different. She didn't know any men who were spiritual in their beliefs.

She'd never met a man like Rafe.

She was about to ask him about his childhood and whether he was raised with faith from a young age, when she heard a loud shriek and loud excited barking.

"Mommy! Fire! The Christmas tree is on fire!"

EIGHT

Fire? Kayla bolted toward the trap door leading out of the attic, but Rafe got there first. He swung down, hitting the ground below with a solid thunk. She climbed down seconds behind him, her heart jumping into her throat as piercing sound of a smoke alarm split the air.

She flew down the stairs to the main level of the house, and the lower she got, the thicker the heavy scent of smoke. The irritant made her cough as she frantically searched for her daughter. "Brianna?" she called hoarsely. "Where are you?"

"Mom-my?" Brianna was coughing, too, and a cold tingle of fear trickled down her spine. Brianna's asthma always seemed worse in the winter, what would happen now with Brianna being in a smoke-filled room?

"I've got Brianna and Clyde. I'm taking them outside," Rafe called out in his deep voice. "Kayla, can you see the door?"

The smoke burned her eyes and she blinked rapidly, trying to see through the haze. Her eyes teared up and she could just make out the open door. "Yes. Ellen? Are you here? Ellen? Where are you?"

"Kayla, get outside!" This time Rafe's voice held a

distinct note of anger. "I'll find Ellen. Brianna needs you."

She couldn't argue, especially when she could still hear Brianna coughing. She found herself praying as she fumbled for the door. *Dear Lord, please keep Ellen safe. And please help Brianna. Please?*

Fresh air welcomed her as she stumbled outside. Still coughing, tears streaming down her face, she looked for Brianna. A safe distance from the house, she saw Rafe holding her daughter in his arms and Clyde barking at his feet, so she hurried over.

"She's coughing a lot," Rafe muttered, his voice full of concern. "The smoke is really bothering her."

"She has asthma," Kayla murmured, taking Brianna into her arms. "She needs her inhaler."

"Where is it?"

"There's one in my purse, it's on the kitchen table."

"I'll find it." Rafe dashed back inside the house.

"Can't breathe," Brianna gasped between coughs. The air in Kayla's own chest squeezed painfully when she could actually hear the wheezing in Brianna's lungs.

"Rafe is getting your inhaler, sweetheart," she said, smoothing a hand down Brianna's back. "Try to relax. Fighting to breathe is only going to make things worse. Here, breathe down into your shirt." She knew from past experience that sometimes breathing into a paper bag helped to ease the coughing. Maybe trapping the air at least a little would help.

"Can't Mommy."

Full of anguish, she could only watch Brianna struggle to catch her breath. Where was Rafe? They needed to call 911. Her daughter needed an ambulance. Now.

"Kayla?" She turned toward Ellen's voice, grateful her mother-in-law had gotten out of the house, too. "Here," she said, thrusting the inhaler into Kayla's hands. "Rafe called 911 and gave me Brianna's inhaler."

Gratefully, she pinched the inhaler between her fingers and set Brianna on her feet. "Here, Brianna. Take two puffs."

Brianna took two breaths from the inhaler and her coughing got a little better, but didn't stop completely. Kayla glanced up at Ellen. "I need to take her to the hospital."

Rafe came over, carrying their winter coats. "Here, put these on. I used the fire extinguisher from the kitchen and managed to put the fire out. It was pretty much centered in the Christmas tree. But the fire department and an ambulance are on the way. Apparently a nearby motorist saw the fire and called it in." He glanced down at Brianna. "With the ambulance on the way, our best bet is to stay put. They'll be here any minute."

"Thank you," Kayla murmured, pulling her coat on and then helping Brianna with hers. Clyde finally calmed down but Brianna was still struggling to breathe. "Try another puff on your inhaler," she suggested.

A horrible coughing fit gripped Brianna and the little girl nearly doubled over, gasping for air. Kayla could only watch helplessly as her daughter struggled to take a deep breath. The smoke had caused an asthma attack that was the worst she'd seen in two years. Brianna needed a breathing treatment and fast.

The welcoming sound of sirens reassured her that help was on the way. When Brianna's coughing fit ended, she urged her daughter to use the inhaler again.

Soon her front yard was engulfed in chaos. Several firefighters dragged a long hose attached to a water truck into her house to make sure the fire was indeed out. Being so far away from the city, and in the woods, there were no fire hydrants nearby. Another firefighter came over to see what he could do for Brianna.

"Here, let's try some oxygen," he said, placing a small face mask over Brianna's nose and mouth.

The oxygen helped, but when the firefighter used his stethoscope to listen to her lungs, he glanced up at Kayla and shook his head. "Still wheezing pretty bad. She needs a medicated breathing treatment."

"I know," Kayla whispered.

Just then the ambulance pulled into the driveway. Thankfully, Kayla waited as the two EMTs hurried over. "What's going on?" the tall male asked.

"My daughter is having a severe asthma attack. Do you have access to albuterol breathing treatments?" Kayla asked.

"Yes, we do." The female EMT hunkered down near Brianna, making eye contact with the little girl. "Will you let me carry you to the ambulance? We have medicine in there that will help your breathing."

Brianna's eyes were wide but she gave a quick nod, still not able to talk very much. Kayla followed Brianna into the ambulance, unwilling to let her daughter out of her sight.

"Here you go," the female EMT said, handing Brianna the mouthpiece once she'd set up the BIRD respirator. Brianna knew the drill well enough to know how to clamp her lips around the mouthpiece and to suck in several deep breaths.

The medicine worked, although every so often Brianna began coughing again. The two EMTs glanced at each other and Kayla sensed they were still concerned.

"Ma'am, we'd feel better if a doctor at the local hospital examined your daughter," the male EMT said as the female EMT nodded her agreement.

Kayla didn't hesitate. "That's fine. I'd feel better, too."

"Good. We'll take off then. You can sit back here with your daughter if you'd like."

"Okay." She moved to sit down next to Brianna, but then glanced back outside the ambulance doors. "Rafe?" she called, snagging his attention from where he was in deep discussion with the firefighter. He immediately crossed over to her, looking up at her expectantly. "Would you put Clyde in the basement and then bring Ellen to meet us at the hospital?"

"Of course." His expression was one of concern. "We'll be right behind you."

"Thanks," she murmured, realizing how fortunate she was to have Rafe at her side during a crisis like this. The very first time Brianna had suffered a severe asthma attack, Jeremy had been out on the lake and she'd been alone. Having Rafe to share the burden was reassuring. Less frightening.

The male EMT closed the back doors to the ambulance and then climbed into the driver's seat.

The drive to the hospital didn't take long, and Kayla was relieved that Brianna seemed to have her breathing under control by the time they arrived. Still, Kayla couldn't relax completely until the doctor had examined Brianna.

The two EMTs wheeled Brianna on their stretcher into one of the empty rooms in the small hospital emergency department. A nurse and a doctor came in immediately.

Kayla handed her daughter into their care, even though it wasn't easy to give her up to stand back, keeping out of the way. When Dr. Graham, as he'd introduced himself, listened to Brianna's lungs, she watched his face closely.

"So what happened to kick-start this asthma attack?" he asked calmly as he pulled the stethoscope buds out of his ears.

"Smoke from a fire in the Christmas tree," she explained quickly.

"Hmm," Dr. Graham murmured.

"Pulse ox still hovering around eighty-eight percent," the nurse said, reading the number off a nearby machine that monitored Brianna's oxygen level with a clothespin device clipped on her index finger. "And she's a little tachy, heart rate one hundred twenty-two."

"Keep her oxygen at two liters per minute for now," Dr. Graham instructed. He turned toward Kayla. "I'd like to keep your daughter here for observation for a bit, if that's all right with you. Smoke inhalation on top of asthma can be very serious. Her oxygen saturation should be above ninety percent. I'd hate to discharge her only to have her suffer a relapse."

A relapse? Her eyes widened in horror. "Of course she'll stay for as long as you recommend. Give her whatever treatments you think are best." Being self-employed, her medical insurance coverage was nonexistent, but she wasn't going to quibble about money at a time like this. Brianna's health was far more important than being in debt and besides, she was pretty sure the hospital would set up some sort of payment plan.

At least, she hoped so.

Rafe and Ellen arrived moments later. Dr. Graham and the nurse left, talking in low tones, no doubt about their next steps. Ellen reached over to give Brianna a hug. Rafe stood back, but she could see the concern reflected in his black eyes.

"She'll be fine," Kayla murmured, flashing a weak smile as he came to stand beside her. "They want to observe her for a while to make sure she's okay."

Rafe took her hand and she grasped onto him gratefully. He bowed his head and closed his eyes. "Dear Lord, thank You for protecting us from the fire. And thank You for restoring Brianna's health, Amen."

"Amen," Kayla whispered, humbled by Rafe's quiet, yet heartfelt prayer. The idea of God watching over them was very reassuring. Somehow, she didn't find it at all difficult to believe God had protected Brianna when she needed Him the most.

Rafe's fingers tightened briefly on hers and she couldn't help thinking again how different Rafe was from any man she'd ever known. His spirituality awed her. He was strong physically, but he was also strong emotionally, too. She let out a tiny sigh and leaned her head against Rafe's shoulder. He instantly wrapped his arm around her waist, hugging her close, silently offering support and comfort.

Kayla inhaled Rafe's musky scent, relaxing for the first time since she'd heard Brianna shouting about the fire. She tipped her head back to glance up at Rafe's handsome profile, trying not to compare him to Jeremy, knowing it was hardly fair. Just because Jeremy didn't have a spiritual side, didn't make him less of a husband and father.

Yet she couldn't deny Rafe had given her a glimpse of a new future. One that offered a higher level of fulfillment if she followed the path leading to God. She knew Rafe would show her the way.

And she discovered she wanted to see what this new future might hold for her, very much.

* * *

When Brianna was discharged, Rafe carried her out to his jeep, tucking her into the backseat beside Ellen. Kayla took the passenger seat beside him and he couldn't ignore the distinctive family-like feel to the atmosphere as he drove back to Kayla's bed-and-breakfast.

He still remembered those fearful moments when he worried he wouldn't get everyone out of the house in time. He'd counted on God's support and had been very thankful when they'd emerged essentially unscathed.

Except for Brianna's asthma attack. Watching the little girl struggle to breathe had been horrible. If he could have offered up his lungs for her, he would have. Talk about feeling totally helpless. Not something he cared to repeat anytime soon.

He'd never been happier than when the breathing treatments had finally kicked in, bringing Brianna's oxygen levels above ninety percent. After another hour of observation, Dr. Graham declared her ready for discharge.

The firefighters had been discussing the source of the fire when he'd left to follow Kayla. They were trying to rule out arson, but he hadn't stayed to hear what theory they'd finally decided upon. Unfortunately, when he pulled into Kayla's driveway, they'd already left the scene. He could only assume they'd be back.

The burnt Christmas tree was lying in the front of the yard, where the firemen had dragged it. The branches were burned but there had been more smoke than anything because of the water in the tree stand keeping it moist. Dusk was starting to fall, but he left his headlights on and peered closely at the worst part of the burnt tree, down by the base of the trunk. The firefighters had noticed it was odd for the fire to have started there, so close to the water tray.

He wrinkled his nose. What was that smell? Gasoline? He hunkered down next to the tree, practically putting his nose right on top of the charred tree trunk. The acrid scent burned his nostrils. Yep, definitely gasoline.

A chill raised the hairs on the back of his neck. Gasoline would explain why the fire had started where it had. And also confirmed the fire had been set on purpose.

"Kayla, wait!" Rafe jumped up and jogged over to where Kayla was about to enter the house.

An unsecured house, as the security system was not engaged.

"What?" she asked, stopping on the porch and turning to face him. Brianna was draped over her shoulder, the little girl's eyelids drooping from sheer exhaustion.

"Go back to my jeep. Both of you," he said, including Ellen who stood beside Kayla. "The house isn't locked and I'm afraid the fire might have been set on purpose."

"What?" Ellen looked aghast. "On purpose? Why?"

Kayla paled, but instantly spun around to head wordlessly back to the jeep. Rafe hurried alongside, wanting to make sure they were safely tucked inside the jeep before he headed into the house.

Should he call his commanding officer? For a moment his fingers hesitated on the phone. No, first he'd go inside, see if anyone had been there.

Might still be there.

Rafe leaned into the driver's door and started the jeep's engine, setting the thermostat on full blast because he could hear Kayla's teeth chattering. He wasn't sure her shivering was from the cold, more likely from hearing his theory about how the fire might not have been an accident. Then he reached over and pulled his weapon out of the glove compartment. He heard Kayla's harshly indrawn breath.

He locked his gaze on hers, reading the fear and apprehension clouding her gaze. He wanted to reassure her, but what could he say? The whole situation reeked of a setup.

Had he imagined the faint whiff of gasoline? No way. For all he knew, the firefighters had already deemed the fire as arson, too. They'd no doubt be back to talk to Kayla if that was the case.

"Everything is going to be fine," he murmured. "Roll up the windows and lock the jeep. If anything happens, drive out of here and head straight to the coast guard home port substation. Understand?"

"Yes," she whispered faintly. "I understand. But I'm not leaving without you, Rafe. Why don't we just go now?"

He hesitated, seeing the wisdom in her question. But other than his gut instinct and the faint odor of gasoline, what did he have? Nothing. Not yet. "We will. Just give me a couple of minutes to look around inside, okay?"

She frowned but then nodded. "Okay."

Stepping away from the vehicle, he waited until Kayla had rolled up the windows and he'd heard the door locks click in. Satisfied, he headed for the house.

At the front door, he paused and listened. The absent light on the security system seemed to mock him from the white panel beside the door. He hadn't thought twice about following Kayla and Brianna to the hospital, leaving the firefighters here and the property basically unsecured. Had that been part of the plan?

Had Gregory Landrum, or whatever his name was, used this as a ruse to get rid of them?

Reaching out, he twisted the door knob and opened the door. The interior of the house was quiet. Too quiet.

Clyde wasn't barking at all.

Had Greg Landrum hurt the dog?

Rafe slipped inside the house, methodically making his way through the great room, around to the kitchen. When he opened the door leading to Kayla's private suite of rooms, a loud screech of a rusty door hinge made his heart jump.

Clyde began to bark from the depths of the basement.

He let out his breath in relief. At least the dog was okay. Figuring the dog might help roust an intruder, he went over and opened the basement door, allowing Clyde to come up. The dog greeted him like a long-lost friend, although they'd only been gone a few hours.

Clyde didn't leave Rafe's side as he walked farther down the hall, prepared for anything. He'd never been in Kayla's private space and he felt like an intruder as he opened one bedroom door after another. Brianna's room, Ellen's room and the bathroom seemed basically untouched from what he could tell.

He came upon Kayla's bedroom last. But unlike the other two rooms, this room wasn't neat and tidy. Her personal items were tossed everywhere and her mattress was slit wide open.

The place had been ransacked. Badly.

Obviously Landrum had already been here. And it was very possible, he'd found exactly what he'd been looking for.

NINE

Rafe stared at the mess for a long minute, knowing how this latest turn of events would upset Kayla. Then he spun on his heel and continued searching through the rest of the house.

Whoever had been there was gone. But just the fact that their intruder had gotten this close bothered him. Had Landrum followed them yesterday? Or was he even right now holed up someplace nearby, watching them? It was hard to imagine the guy Kayla had described as camping out in the cold woods, but anything was possible.

And worse, how had Landrum sneaked into the house to set the fire in the Christmas tree while they were up in the attic? He thought back and realized that Kayla hadn't set the security system as they were waiting for Ellen and Brianna to return. He should have insisted, since that brief window of time must have been enough for Landrum to sneak in to start the fire.

It was his fault that Brianna had almost stopped breathing.

He closed his eyes on a wave of despair. Thankfully, God was watching over them or this entire situation could have ended much worse.

No more mistakes, he vowed. No more distractions. Rafe would keep his concentration centered on this case and would absolutely follow his gut instincts from now on.

Nothing else had been disturbed other than Kayla's bedroom. Did that mean Landrum had found what he was searching for? Or would he be back to finish the job?

Rafe didn't like either theory.

And regardless, he needed to get Kayla and Brianna out of there as soon as possible.

He headed back out to the car where Kayla, Ellen and Brianna waited, with Clyde at his heels. Kayla rolled down the window when he approached, gazing up at him expectantly. His chest squeezed with the thought of her being in danger.

"We're going to go inside just long enough to pack a bag," he told her brusquely. "Then we're leaving."

"Leaving? What happened?" Kayla asked, her gaze full of trepidation.

"Your bedroom has been tossed," he said grimly. At her blank look, he clarified, "It's been searched. Someone has been here while we were gone. I'm sorry, Kayla, but your room is a total mess."

"Brianna's, too?" she asked.

"No, the other two rooms weren't touched," Rafe said flatly, trying to hide his anger at the situation. At his failure. "Just yours."

For a long moment she stared at him. "So he found what he was looking for?" she guessed.

"I don't know." He met her gaze squarely. "But whether he did or not doesn't matter. We're not staying long enough to find out."

* * *

Kayla tried to assimilate what Rafe had just told her as she unpeeled her fingers from their tight grip on the steering wheel. She'd been prepared to drive off, as Rafe had ordered her to, even though leaving him behind went against every cell in her being. It seemed like he'd been inside for hours, rather than for the seventeen minutes that had ticked off on the clock dashboard. She'd been so afraid that something had happened to him.

To that end, knowing the only damage was to her bedroom was a relief. Things could be replaced.

Rafe couldn't.

"I want to see for myself," she said, glancing over at Brianna, who was sleeping beside her, as she hit the button to unlock the doors.

Rafe pulled the driver's door open. "Fine. But we're only going inside long enough to pack some things. I'll carry Brianna."

She didn't argue when he swept her daughter into his arms as if she weighed nothing more than a feather. Her knees were still rubbery after everything she'd been through. The fire, the desperate ambulance ride to the hospital and now this. She swallowed her fear and walked inside with Ellen beside her. Her mother-in-law didn't say a word when Kayla headed straight for her bedroom.

In the doorway, she paused, sucking in a harsh breath. *Searched* wasn't the word she would have used. *Destroyed* was the term that came to mind. Her room had been utterly and completely destroyed. Every drawer had been upended, her closet torn apart and her mattress slit open from top to bottom. She momentarily closed her eyes, knowing she should be grateful the damage wasn't worse.

"Rafe's right, Kay," Ellen whispered from behind her. "We need to leave. Right away."

She knew her mother-in-law was right, but at the same time, she couldn't help thinking that they should search the other two rooms while they still had time. What if Gregory Landrum hadn't found what he was looking for? There was still a possibility they could find it first.

She turned and went back to where Rafe had gently placed a still sleeping Brianna on the sofa in the living room. The walls in the corner where the tree had been standing were scorched black from the heat of the fire. But the damage was pretty much confined to the farthest corner of the room, and if not for the stench of smoke that still lingered in the air and the blackened walls, there wasn't much evidence of the fire that had caused Brianna's asthma attack.

"I can't believe she's still asleep," Kayla murmured, kneeling down beside the sofa, and brushing a strand of Brianna's hair from her daughter's pale cheek. "She must be exhausted."

Rafe's gaze was troubled. "Should we be worried about a relapse?"

"It's a possibility," she admitted, glancing up at him. "Rafe, I know we can't stay here tonight, but Brianna was just released from the hospital. Couldn't we let her rest a little before we leave? That way we'd have time to search the other two rooms first. Just in case there is something that the intruder managed to miss."

Rafe clenched his jaw and shook his head. "No. I'm sorry, but my gut is telling me we need to get out of here, now, before anything else happens. Isn't it bad enough that I let my guard down and let Landrum sneak in while we were upstairs in the attic? I know Brianna's exhausted but she can sleep in the car."

She heard the underlying steel in his tone and realized further arguing would be futile. Especially since he was shouldering the responsibility for her mistake. "Actually, Rafe, I'm the one who didn't set the security system when we came in because I was expecting Ellen and Brianna to return at any moment. So stop beating yourself up over this when the fault clearly rests with me."

"No, Kayla, it's not your fault at all. I'm the one who should have reminded you to set the alarm. But enough placing blame. What happened before doesn't matter. Right now, we need to plan our escape. I need you and Ellen to pack a bag, and then pull some stuff together for Brianna. I'll make our reservations at the motel, then take care of my things and pack some food."

Kayla gave in. "All right," she agreed, glancing over at Ellen who hovered in the doorway. "Is that all right with you?" she asked, belatedly realizing they'd been discussing the next steps without including her mother-in-law.

Ellen flushed and dropped her gaze, guiltily. "Actually, Kayla, my sister Irene called while we were in the emergency department with Brianna. She's being released from the hospital earlier than originally planned. If you don't mind, I'd like to catch the first available flight to Phoenix, Arizona, instead."

Kayla swallowed her urge to protest. She'd known this day was coming, that Ellen would leave to go stay with her sister, she just hadn't expected it to be so soon.

As if sensing her hesitancy, Ellen glanced at her with a pleading gaze. "I'm sorry, Kayla, but Irene needs me."

"I know," Kayla murmured, trying to force a smile. She'd been counting on Ellen being a buffer between her and Rafe. A selfish thought considering how she'd known Ellen's plans all along were to only stay a few days, until her sister's release from the hospital. "It's fine. Of course you need to go to your sister. I'm sure Rafe won't mind dropping you off at the airport."

"No, I don't mind," Rafe agreed.

"Kayla, maybe you and Brianna should come to Phoenix with me," Ellen said anxiously. "No one would think to look for you there. You and Brianna would be safe for sure."

"Irene lives in a small apartment in a retirement community, remember?" Kayla pointed out, glancing over at Rafe who was watching the discussion with a frown. Did he want her to go? "No children allowed. And even if the rules could be broken, there wouldn't be enough room for us."

"There's a hotel nearby," Ellen protested.

But Kayla was already shaking her head. "I can't afford a hotel, Ellen. Or plane tickets for that matter. And honestly, I don't want to leave. This place," she swept a hand around, encompassing the bed-and-breakfast, "This is all I have left of Jeremy. I need to stay close by."

Rafe knew he was being selfish as an overwhelming relief washed over him when Kayla declined her mother-in-law's offer to go to Phoenix. She and Brianna might be safe in Arizona, but then again, maybe not. If she became the target, it wouldn't be difficult for Landrum or any of his underlings to figure out where she'd gone.

And he couldn't deny, he wanted Kayla and Brianna close by so he could keep an eye on them.

"Okay it's settled," Rafe said, breaking the sudden silence. "We'll drive Ellen to the airport before I take you and Brianna someplace safe."

"Don't forget Clyde," Brianna said with a yawn from the sofa. "We have to take Clyde with us."

Rafe glanced at Brianna, noting that she looked much better after her short nap. "And Clyde," he amended with a smile. "How are you feeling?"

"I'm tired." Brianna yawned again but then pried her eyes open. "Are we going on a trip?"

"Yes, we're going on a little trip. How about if we go into your room to pack your things?" Kayla asked, glancing up at Rafe. He understood she didn't want Brianna to know about the mess in her room. "I'll help, all right?"

"Okay," Brianna agreed, scrambling down from the sofa.

"Why don't you let me help Brianna while you get some of your things together first?" Ellen said, stepping forward.

Kayla hesitated, but then nodded, her expression grateful. He could hear the women speaking in low tones as they walked toward the kitchen, heading to Kayla's private rooms. He wanted to offer his help, but sensed Kayla would be uncomfortable if he were to go through her personal items.

He took the stairs two at a time, heading to his room and quickly pulling his stuff together. He called the Willow Grove motel to reserve two rooms. When those arrangements were finished, he made sure to grab his laptop computer, knowing he had more searching to do. When his phone rang, he glanced at the display, realizing his errant partner was finally checking in.

"Evan? Where are you?" he asked, trying not to sound accusing. Truthfully, he hadn't even thought about his partner since leaving home port substation.

"I'm tailing Yancy. He's moored for now, but he's loading up on fuel as if he's preparing for a long trip. And I'm pretty sure he has a passenger on board. I'm going to stay with him, I think he might be our guy." Evan's voice echoed with excited anticipation.

Rafe took a deep breath. "Okay, Evan, but don't get too close. Or better yet, call for some backup, just in case. If he discovers you behind him, he could take you out without warning."

"Rafe, trust me. I know what I'm doing," Evan said confidently.

Rafe wished he could be so sure. "Call for backup," he repeated. "And one more thing, did you talk to Charlie Turkow?"

"No, I didn't talk to Charlie. Look Rafe, I have to go. I'll check in with you later." Evan disconnected the line before Rafe could say another word.

He stared at his phone for a moment. Should he warn Luke? Evan wouldn't be happy, but Rafe couldn't be certain that his partner would really listen to his advice. Batting down the wave of guilt, he made the call. His commanding officer didn't answer, so he left a terse message, informing Luke of the latest break-in at Kayla's and then mentioning Evan's location and his need for backup. Afterward, he felt better.

At least he'd done his best to protect his partner. Now if he could manage to keep Kayla and Brianna safe, he'd be content.

Hauling his duffel bag downstairs, he set it near the

front door and then nearly tripped over the dog as he went into the kitchen to rummage for food. They'd need enough for at least a day or two to be on the safe side. He added Clyde's food and water bowls to the pile of things they needed to take.

Searching through Kayla's cupboards, though, revealed that she didn't have a lot of staples. He took a few items, the bread so it wouldn't go stale, peanut butter and jelly for Brianna, along with a few other items from the fridge that might go bad if left behind, but that was all. He knew Kayla's financial situation was serious, so he'd stop at a grocery store to pick up the rest of the items they might need. At least there was a half bag of dog food left so he put that over by the doorway as well.

Kayla came out of her bedroom with a small suitcase. "At least he didn't destroy my clothes," she said.

"I'll replace your mattress, Kayla," he reassured her. "And the repairs from the fire. Once this is over, I'll take care of everything."

"It's okay, Rafe. I have homeowner's insurance."

He frowned. "I insist."

She rolled her eyes and took her suitcase over to set it next to his duffel bag. "Just a few more minutes and we should be ready to go."

"No problem," he murmured. She went back to Brianna's room, to get her daughter's things. He could tell how much she hated having to leave her home. For a moment, a prickle of doubt niggled into his resolve. Were they better off staying here, locked inside the house with the security system on?

No, the fire was proof of how far this guy would go to get them out of here. What's to say he won't get more desperate? His first instinct was the right one. They'd get out now, while they could.

"Mommy, I want to take my album!" Brianna's voice rose with a rare fit of temper. Rafe took a few steps down the hall, willing to lend a hand if needed.

"Brianna, it's not like we're going away for weeks," Kayla said in exasperation.

"I don't care." The door burst open and Brianna came flying through, barreling headfirst into Rafe.

"Whoa, slow down," he said, reaching for her.

The photo album she carried hit the floor and skated across the linoleum, hitting the base of cabinets hard enough to knock several pictures loose.

"Okay, fine. Bring the album." Kayla came out behind her, carrying Brianna's suitcase and wearing a harried expression. Ellen wheeled her suitcase over to place it near the rest of the bags, and Clyde pounced on the scattered photos as if this were some sort of new game. Rafe knelt down to pick up the photos before Clyde could damage them.

"What in the world?" he muttered, when he picked up the first photograph. It wasn't a family picture of Brianna, Kayla or Jeremy as he'd expected. Instead this photograph was taken down by the lakefront, but the stranger in the picture was climbing into one of Schroeder's charter fishing boats.

With a frown he picked up the rest of the loose photographs, five in all, noting they were all similar, photographs of men near or in the act of climbing aboard one of the boats. When he came to the last photo, he recognized the man near the boat.

Bruce Pappas. The first criminal suspected of fleeing the country to Canada through one of Schroeder's boats.

"What is it?" Kayla asked crossing over to see what he was staring at.

"Evidence," Rafe said slowly, his tone full of amazement. He lifted his head to capture Kayla's gaze. "I think Brianna found the evidence Schroeder hid in your house."

TEN

"What?" Kayla stared at Rafe, her expression appalled. "Bill stashed those photographs in my daughter's photo album? What was he thinking, putting Brianna in danger like that?"

Rafe couldn't disagree with Kayla's frustration. A deep sense of foreboding cloaked his excitement at finally having a break in the case. The fact that these photographs were still here only meant that Landrum would be coming back to continue his search. And soon. They needed to get out of here now. "I doubt he thought of it like that, Kayla," he said, trying to soothe her distress. "I'm sure he never realized he was being watched and followed."

Kayla scowled darkly. "Well, he should have considered the possibility. The nerve of him. When I think about how sick Brianna was with her asthma in the emergency department because of what he's done..." She clenched her hands into fists, unable to finish her thought out loud.

"Mommy? What's wrong?" Brianna asked, sensing the tension in the room.

Rafe watched as Kayla forced a smile on her face, relaxed her fists and shoved her anger aside for her daughter's sake. "Nothing's wrong, Bree. I'm just a little cranky, that's all. Get Clyde's leash, will you?" She turned toward Rafe. "Is there anything else we need or are we ready to go?"

"We're ready." He didn't want to panic her by mentioning his fears of Landrum returning. The sooner they got out of here, the better. "Give me a minute to get everything packed into the jeep. Ellen, I'm going to leave your suitcase for last, since we're dropping you off at the airport first."

"That's fine," Ellen murmured, her expression troubled.

Rafe took the photographs and slid them into his laptop case before hauling the first load of suitcases out to the jeep. He made two trips, but soon he had everything neatly stored in the back. Brianna took Clyde out one last time while Kayla set the security system on the house. When everyone, including the dog, was safe inside the jeep, they were ready to go.

Rafe noticed how Kayla twisted in her seat, watching the house fade away behind them as he headed out of her long winding driveway. He wanted to reassure her that with this new lead they'd have the mastermind of the criminal smuggling ring behind bars very soon but at the same time, he couldn't deny the danger, especially now that they'd found the evidence Schroeder had hidden. Landrum obviously wanted these pictures. No wonder he'd taken all the photographs from the boxes of Jeremy's things.

Kayla looked upset, so he reached over and took her hand in his, giving it a small, reassuring squeeze. "Everything is going to be fine," he told her softly. "God will watch over us."

"I know." Her sincere tone and tremulous smile warmed his heart.

He kept a keen eye on the road behind him to ensure they weren't being followed. As he gained distance from Kayla's bed-and-breakfast, he slowly began to relax. The worst of the danger was over. And he couldn't ignore the sense of satisfaction, knowing they finally had something to go on.

Of course, Kayla's and Brianna's safety needed to come first. But now that he had the photographs, he couldn't help but think they could blow the case wide open. Evan was trailing Karl Yancy and if the recluse was the mastermind behind the criminal smuggling ring, they could put the lid on this case very soon.

Silently, he vowed to do whatever was necessary in order to have Kayla and Brianna home in time for Christmas.

Kayla took several deep breaths in a vain attempt to relax. The crushing fear she'd experienced when she'd realized Bill had exposed her daughter to danger still weighed heavily on her shoulders. Even with Rafe holding on to her hand, she had trouble relaxing.

Verse six of the first Psalm flashed in her memory. *For the Lord watches over the way of the righteous, but the way of the wicked will perish.* Her fear slipped away and she was finally able to relax.

Bill was gone and he would answer to God for his sins. Hanging on to her fear and anger was useless. She needed to focus her energies on remaining positive. Brianna was fine now. The crisis of her asthma attack was over. Rafe was right in that God was watching over them.

She needed to have faith. Practice makes perfect, she thought with a sigh.

Everyone in the jeep was unusually silent as Rafe sped toward the Green Bay airport. When he pulled up in front of the passenger drop-off gate, Kayla stepped out to give her mother-in-law one last hug while Brianna held on to the dog to prevent him from racing out, too.

"Oh, Kayla, are you sure you won't change your mind about coming with me?" Ellen asked fretfully. "I'll pay for your plane tickets and your hotel."

For a brief moment, the idea was tempting. But her mother-in-law lived on a fixed income and even if she had the money, Kayla knew she wouldn't go.

She couldn't leave Rafe. Or the house Jeremy had built for them. "I'm sure," Kayla whispered. "We'll be fine, I promise. You concentrate on taking care of Irene, all right?"

Ellen nodded, but she didn't look happy as she made her way to the ticket counter. Rafe waited patiently as Kayla got back into the car before he pulled away from the curb.

"I—uh, thought we'd stop for groceries before heading to the motel," Rafe said, breaking the silence. "The rooms are equipped with a small refrigerator and a microwave, so we'll have to keep it simple."

Her smile was wry. "I've been keeping it simple for a while now, so that's no problem," she assured him.

He cast a sideways glance in her direction, but didn't say anything more until they pulled into a grocery store near the airport. She was surprised when Rafe pulled some money out of his wallet and handed it to her. "Will you pick up a few things that you know Brianna will like? I'll come inside with you, but I need to call my commanding officer to let him know about these photographs we found."

Taking his money felt wrong, but since her wallet was pretty much empty she shoved her pride aside and reluctantly accepted the money.

Clyde looked pathetically forlorn when they locked him inside the jeep. Inside the store, Brianna seemed to be back to normal, only a little subdued as Kayla pushed the grocery cart through the store aisles. As they picked out various items, from soup to oatmeal, Kayla listened to Rafe's side of the conversation with his boss.

"We found the evidence Schroeder left in Kayla's B and B," he said, getting straight to the point. "A half dozen photographs. I recognize Bruce Pappas and I'm sure the other criminals who have escaped are in these other photographs, too. We just need to match them up with their mug shots."

There was a short pause, as Rafe listened to whatever Luke was saying in response.

"Yeah, a list of names and dates would have been nice, too bad Schroeder didn't package everything up in a nice bundle for us. I'm not sure why he hid the photos, unless he'd gotten cold feet and was looking for a way out. Unfortunately, his attempt to get out didn't work since he ended up in the lake instead. Any word from Evan?"

It didn't take long for Kayla to pick up the few items they'd need and as she went through the checkout line, she heard Rafe finish up with his boss.

"I'll find Charlie Turkow tomorrow morning, show him the sketch Kayla did of our suspect and see what happens. Maybe I'll even show him the photographs. I can't help thinking that old man knows a lot more about what's going on than he's been willing to tell us. See

you tomorrow." Another pause, then, "Yes, sir, I will."
Rafe snapped his phone shut as she finished paying the
grocery bill.

"You will what?" she asked curiously as Rafe took
their bags and led the way back out to the jeep.

He glanced at her, his expression serious. "Take care
of you and Brianna."

She couldn't hide her surprise. "Your boss asked you
to do that? Take care of us?"

"Of course." He opened the back if the jeep to set the
groceries inside. "The coast guard is all about protecting
innocent civilians."

His words, innocent civilians, echoed in her mind as
she climbed back into the passenger seat. What if that
wasn't entirely true? She and Brianna were innocent of
course, but after that, she wasn't as certain. She'd been
so upset with Bill for dragging her into this mess, but
maybe, just maybe he'd chosen to hide the evidence in
her house because of Jeremy.

Was it possible her husband was more involved in the
criminal smuggling business than she'd realized? Was
it possible he wasn't nearly as innocent as she wanted
to believe?

Kayla gazed at the rather run-down exterior of the
Willow Grove Motel while Rafe went inside to book
them two rooms. The owner had tried to cheer the place
up with holiday lights strung along the outside frame,
but from her perspective, the lights only highlighted
the neglect. At least from what she could see, the place
was fairly clean, and she told herself that was all that
mattered.

They'd stopped for dinner at a local fast-food restaurant on the way. Brianna had kept herself entertained

during the ride between playing with Clyde and her small handheld video game.

"Can we go inside now, Mommy?" Brianna asked for the third time.

"Not until Mr. Rafe brings us a key, remember?"

"What's taking him so long?" Brianna demanded, impatiently. "We've been in the car for *hours*."

They'd only been in the car for an hour and ten minutes and that was only because they'd had to backtrack in order to drop Ellen off at the airport. But she didn't bother to correct Brianna because just then, Rafe came back outside, ducking his head against the wind.

"Chance of snow tonight," he said by way of greeting. "Not much, just a dusting but enough to make the roads slick."

"Yay," Brianna cried happily from the backseat. "I was hoping for a white Christmas."

Personally, Kayla had been enjoying the unusually warm December weather. Snow was pretty, except when you had to drive around in it.

Rafe drove around the small building and pulled up to rooms five and six in the row of motel rooms. The overhang of the room offered little protection from the cold as he used the key to open her room first, and then his own.

Brianna jumped out of the back, holding Clyde's leash. "Make sure he goes to the bathroom," Kayla warned.

"I will." Brianna didn't seem nearly as bothered by the cold.

The small motel room was clean and had a connecting door to Rafe's room. Brianna brought Clyde inside and then bounced excitedly on one of the two double beds as Rafe hauled in their bags.

"Brianna, get down," she warned before looking over at Rafe. "Thanks for your help."

"No problem." He glanced around, gesturing to the door connecting their rooms. "I'm right on the other side if you need anything. I'll leave my side open, just in case."

"I'm sure we'll be fine," she said, injecting confidence in her tone. A wide yawn sneaked up on her. "It's been a long day."

"I'll check in with you in the morning." Rafe added, "Before I leave to meet Luke, all right?"

"Sounds good." She didn't want to think about how she'd manage to keep Brianna and Clyde entertained during the long day in the confines of the motel. It was on the tip of her tongue to ask if they could come along, but then she remembered he was also going to talk to Charlie Turkow, too.

She'd manage to keep Brianna and Clyde entertained, somehow.

"Good night, Kayla," he murmured in a low husky voice. For a moment she was mesmerized by his intense dark eyes as a subtle awareness shimmered between them. Finally he turned away, breaking the intangible connection. "Good night, *mi nina*," he said to Brianna. "Listen to your mother, understand?"

"Good night, Mr. Rafe," Brianna said, rushing over to clutch him around the knees. He bent down to smooth a hand over her daughter's mink-brown hair.

Kayla watched the obvious closeness that had grown between Brianna and Rafe, but she didn't voice her concerns. All along, she'd been worried about Brianna being hurt when Rafe went back to his regular coast guard duties. Yet at the same time, she couldn't imagine being here without him.

And she knew with soul-wrenching certainty that Brianna wasn't the only one who would be hurt when Rafe finally left. Despite her efforts to keep her distance, her emotions were already involved. She liked being with Rafe. Not only did he make her feel safe, he brought a spiritual connection as well.

She cared about him.

Too much for her own good.

Rafe did a sweep around the motel on foot, making sure there was nothing suspicious or out of place before using his key to access his room. He crossed over to unlock his side of the connecting door so that Kayla could reach him if needed.

He quickly set up his computer and began doing some cross-referencing with the photographs he'd found in Brianna's picture album. Before he met with his boss in the morning, he wanted to have the identities of the men in the photos confirmed.

His previous searches on Charlie Turkow hadn't revealed anything that might explain the guy's bad attitude toward the coast guard. No negative stories or interactions with any crew members that he could find.

There were a few thumps from the other side of the connecting door as Kayla and Brianna got settled in for the night. He'd gotten choked up when Brianna had clutched him around the knees, especially when he'd caught a glimpse of the longing in Kayla's eyes and it had taken him several moments to pull himself together.

It was time to tell Kayla the truth about the circumstances surrounding the deaths of his wife and stillborn son. With a guilty start, he remembered wanting to explain how he'd been responsible for what had happened, but the fire had interrupted them before he could explain.

And she needed to understand. As much as he cared about Kayla and Brianna, he couldn't be the husband and father they deserved. She'd realize why once he told her what he'd done.

The grim realization kept him up until the wee hours of the morning as he worked diligently on the case that would soon bring this forced closeness to an end.

The next morning, Rafe's eyes were gritty with lack of sleep, but he ignored the discomfort as he quickly showered and dressed for his upcoming meeting with his boss and hopefully, a face-to-face conversation with Charlie Turkow.

When a door opened and closed loudly from next door, he rushed over to yank his open, relieved to find Kayla bundled up in her coat taking the dog outside.

"Everything all right?" he asked when she glanced over at him.

"Yes, we're fine," Kayla said cheerfully. He was amazed and humbled at how she always seemed to take everything he threw at her in stride without a single complaint. She certainly hadn't deserved to be dragged into this mess. "I realized this morning that you gave me all the food, so when you're hungry, let me know."

As if on cue his stomach rumbled and he had to laugh. "I will."

When he knocked on their connecting door, she opened it up and handed him a steaming plastic bowl of instant oatmeal. "Thanks," he said, taking the dish gratefully. "I'm going to leave in about ten minutes, is there anything you need me to get while I'm out?"

"Not that I can think of," she admitted. "Is it all right

if I take Brianna and Clyde out for a short walk? I'm afraid it's going to be a long day for them."

Rafe hesitated, debating. He was sure they hadn't been followed and Luke was the only other person who knew where he'd taken Kayla. He trusted his boss with his life. "A short walk should be fine," he agreed. "Keep your cell phone with you so that I can get in touch with you if I need to."

"I will. Thanks, Rafe."

He nodded and shut the door, quickly wolfing down his oatmeal. He grabbed his laptop, the photographs, and his notes describing each of the criminal's identities and the dates they'd disappeared.

The photos confirmed that each of the well-known criminals had taken trips on Schroeder's charter fishing boats. One piece of the puzzle had been fit into place, but there were more gaping holes that still needed to be filled.

On the way to the Green Bay substation, he swung past Pelican Point and found Charlie Turkow's boat moored in the dock. With a glance at his watch, he realized he had plenty of time to meet with Charlie first. Better to bring all the information to Luke at once.

He took a copy of Kayla's sketch and the photographs of the criminals who'd all disappeared with him as he approached Charlie's Charter.

"Charlie?" he called out, as he stood near the bow. "Come on, Charlie, I need to talk to you. It's important."

For a moment he feared the old man would ignore him, but suddenly the boat rocked as the older gentleman emerged from below deck. "Are you deaf? I told you I have nothing to say."

Rafe held up the sketch of Gregory Landrum. "Have

you seen this guy, Charlie? We think he's the guy who killed Bill Schroeder."

The flash of fear in the old man's eyes, along with the hasty step backward convinced Rafe that Charlie had recognized him. "So why are you bothering me?"

"Because we need your help to find him," Rafe explained patiently. "Come on, Charlie. I know he's taking criminals out of the United States and hiding them in Canada. I have the evidence right here," Rafe said, holding up the photographs with his other hand.

Charlie's eyes narrowed. "Let me get this straight. You want my help."

Rafe stared at Charlie with a puzzled frown. "Yes, we want your help. Why? What's wrong with that?"

Charlie let out a loud snort of disgust. "What's wrong? You have the nerve to ask? Typical coastie, covering up for your own," he said with a sneer. "Try taking a long hard look in the mirror. You'll find out everything you need to know."

With that parting shot, Charlie spun on his heel and disappeared down below, slamming the cabin door behind him.

ELEVEN

Take a long hard look in the mirror? What in the world was Turkow talking about? Rafe turned away, his mind whirling as he retraced his steps back to his car.

Was Charlie really implying someone from inside the coast guard was involved in the criminal smuggling ring?

Evan's cocky grin popped into his mind. No, that wasn't fair. Just because Evan was young and reckless at times didn't mean he'd betray his oath by participating in something criminal like this.

No, Rafe refused to consider that Evan, or any of his fellow crewmen would lower themselves to the point they'd participate in illegal activity. Charlie must be confused. They already knew the grizzled old charter fishing captain held some sort of grudge against the coast guard.

Obviously, the old man must have seen one of the coast guard cutters tailing Yancy's yacht or his own charter fishing boat for that matter, and had made a wrong assumption.

It was the only explanation that made sense.

But despite his efforts to think positive, Charlie's accusation of how they were protecting their own, kept reverberating in his mind as he made his way to the coast guard substation.

Luke Sanders was waiting in his office. Rafe approached, automatically lifting his hand in a salute.

Luke returned the gesture and then waved his hand impatiently, anxious to get right to the point. "Let's see what you found."

Rafe obliged by spreading the photos over the surface of Luke's glossy desk. "These fell out of Brianna's photo album. I have each man identified as one of the escaped criminals over the past year. You can see from the pictures, every one of them is on one of the Schroeder charter fishing boats."

His commanding officer's gaze sharpened when he picked up the first photo and he let out a low whistle between his teeth. "This is perfect. We have them. We couldn't ask for better proof that Schroeder's charter fishing operation was really part of the underground criminal escape ring." Luke clapped him on the back. "Good work, DeSilva."

Rafe grimaced. "Thank you, sir, but we can't celebrate yet. Schroeder is dead. We need to find the guy in Kayla's sketch, Gregory Landrum. We won't get very far in this investigation if we can't get a hold of one of the key suspects."

Luke nodded thoughtfully. "You're right."

"Now we know why only photographs were taken from the boxes of Jeremy's belongings, though," Rafe mused. "It's as if Landrum knew exactly what he was looking for."

"I agree, Landrum is the key," Luke said. "I updated Evan on the latest in the turn of events last night after sending him the sketch electronically, but he hasn't gotten back to me yet. I don't think Karl Yancy is your guy, but I do think he's involved. There's no way Yancy or Landrum are working alone. The more I think about this the more I believe they're in this mess up to their necks together."

"Yeah, that's the most likely scenario." Rafe hesitated only for a moment, before giving his boss the rest of the information he'd discovered. "I showed the sketch to Charlie Turkow, he definitely recognized the guy and didn't seem too surprised when I told him we suspected the man in the sketch killed Schroeder."

"So the old man does know something," Luke surmised with a snort of satisfaction. "Why isn't he helping us out?"

Rafe blew out a breath, knowing he had to tread carefully here. "Well, sir, he told me to look in the mirror."

"Look in the mirror?" His commanding officer's eyes widened as realization dawned. "He thinks one of us is involved?"

Rafe shrugged. "That's what he said, but it could be that he's noticed our cutters tailing his boat or Yancy's and made a wrong assumption."

"Or he could be right." Luke pinned him with a hard stare. "What do you think? Could there be any truth to the old man's claim?"

"I don't know, sir." Rafe didn't like himself very much at the moment, because he couldn't honestly say no. It was possible that one of the crew was involved, even though he didn't want to go there. And Evan's arrival to the Great Lakes two years ago was almost perfect timing, considering they'd estimated the first criminal escaped eighteen months ago. "How well do you know Evan Marshall? He's the newest member of the team."

Luke scowled. "Evan Marshall came with a solid

work history and strong recommendation from the crew on the northern Atlantic coast. You seriously believe he's guilty?"

"No, sir, that's not what I said." Rafe didn't apologize for the inference, though. "I don't want to think any of our crew might be involved, but we can't ignore the possibility, either."

"There must be a reason that old guy hates us," Luke growled.

"I searched Charlie's background, and I didn't find anything that would give a hint as to why he might hold a grudge against the coast guard."

"Hmm." Luke stared down at the five photos spread over his desk. "Did you check to see if Charlie had ever applied to join the crew? Maybe his grudge comes from being rejected."

Rafe lifted a brow. That was an angle he hadn't considered. "Good point. I didn't see any indication of that in his history, but it's worth going back to check again."

"See that you do." Luke gathered up the photos. "I wish Schroeder would have given us more to go on. If he was really trying to hide evidence to use as leverage, why didn't he hide more detail? Dates, times, new identities of the escaped crooks? Something solid to give us a clue as to where to start looking."

Rafe could sense his commanding officer's frustration and he felt the exact same way. They were so close to breaking the case open. "I know. It's like we're one step closer but not close enough."

"Hopefully Evan will get something on Yancy," Luke said.

"Speaking of Evan, you need to send someone out to back him up, just in case Yancy catches on to him."

His commanding officer looked surprised. "You're not volunteering?"

He wanted to, but he couldn't leave Kayla and Brianna alone. Not yet. Not until he knew they were safe. "No, sir. I've taken Mrs. Wilson and her daughter to a motel, but I can't just leave them to fend for themselves. Not when we know Schroeder hid the evidence in her home. Landrum has already proven how far he'll go in order to get them back."

Luke narrowed his gaze and pursed his lips thoughtfully. "All right, you can stick close to her for another day or so, but if it turns out Yancy is our guy, I'll expect you to join the crew."

Rafe gave a slow nod. He'd always known his duty was going to pull him away from Kayla, but he wasn't ready to leave her. Not yet.

Not until he knew she and Brianna would be safe.

He swallowed hard and turned away.

And prayed he hadn't made a huge mistake by not sending them both on the plane to Arizona with Ellen.

Rafe stopped at Pelican Point before heading back to the motel to meet Kayla. He parked his car in the small lot and walked over to the memorial Bill Schroeder had put up on honor of Kayla's husband, Jeremy.

The memorial had been strategically placed so that it overlooked the lakefront. He glanced down and read the wording engraved on the brass plate:

Placed in honor of Captain Jeremy Allen Wilson. May he rest in peace.

The inscription wasn't particularly profound. Puzzled, he shook his head. All along, he'd been bothered by this. It was the one piece that didn't quite fit. Placing this memorial was a nice gesture, but why had Bill

Schroeder gone through the trouble of putting this up two years after Jeremy's death? Wouldn't he have had better things to do with his time? Especially if he was planning to find a way out of the criminal smuggling ring?

Had the memorial been an excuse to get inside Kayla's house for the sole purpose of hiding the photos? Or had hiding the photos been a last-minute decision, an impulse he'd acted on when the opportunity had presented itself?

He stared at the memorial, trying to understand what Bill Schroeder had been thinking. The design of the memorial was simple, a four-foot high base made out of wood with a two-foot by two-foot square top, also made of wood. A brass plate was screwed into the wooden top, set at an angle so the reader could see the inscription better. But then he frowned when he realized the wooden top was a good three inches thick.

How strange. Wouldn't it have been cheaper to use a half-inch board? Why had Schroeder bothered to make the top so deep?

Deep enough to hide something?

A shaft of anticipation stabbed deep. Rafe couldn't contain a sense of excitement. He jogged back to his jeep, and rummaged in the back. He found a hammer and a crowbar, and took both tools back over to the memorial. He lifted the hammer, pausing only for a moment as he acknowledged Kayla would likely be upset if he tore this apart only to find nothing inside.

But he didn't believe he'd find nothing. Three inches couldn't be a coincidence. The rest of the memorial was built very simply without a lot of expense.

No, he wasn't wrong about this. Lifting the hammer, he slammed it hard against the top of the memorial. It took several blows before he was able to knock it loose. One last hit and the two-foot by two-foot top of the memorial dropped to the ground with a heavy thud.

It didn't break open, so he picked up the crowbar and went to work. Schroeder had built the top of the memorial very sturdy, as if to protect whatever was inside. Finally Rafe pried the top board off.

The hollow top fell apart to reveal a notebook nestled inside. His heart pounding with anticipation, he picked up the notebook and opened it.

Names, dates and new identities of the escapes were all neatly recorded in the spiral notebook.

Luke was right. Schroeder had documented everything.

He tucked the notebook under his arm, picked up the shattered base and hauled everything back to his jeep. He needed to head back to the coast guard substation ASAP. They needed time to go through the entire contents of the notebook.

They finally had exactly what they needed in order to solve the case.

Kayla blew out a breath of frustration. Brianna was bored. They'd played numerous card games, watched a movie on television, and it wasn't even lunchtime.

How in the world would she keep her daughter entertained for the rest of the day?

"Why can't we go outside?" Brianna asked for the zillionth time. "It's sunny and the snow from last night is already melting."

Kayla rose to her feet. Rafe had mentioned they could take a short walk. And Clyde needed to go out again anyway. He was just as antsy as Brianna. "All right, we'll go for a walk. Get Clyde's leash."

"Yay!" Brianna happily pulled on her coat and picked up Clyde's leash from where Kayla had looped it over the back of a chair. When Clyde saw the leash he began jumping around excitedly, knowing he was in for a treat.

Kayla drew on her own coat, double-checking to make sure she had the room key in her pocket. When they were ready, she opened the door and let Brianna and Clyde run outside.

The sound of her daughter's laughter made her smile. Maybe this was exactly what they needed.

With the sun shining high in the sky, the temperature warmed to the point where they could open their coats. She twirled the edge of her knitted scarf as they walked. Very unusual to have temperatures well above freezing during December in Wisconsin, but Kayla wasn't going to complain.

She had no doubt there would be plenty of snow soon enough.

"Maybe this is far enough," Kayla said, halting in her tracks. They'd taken the winding back highway from the motel, toward the small town of Willow Creek, and she'd estimated they'd gone about a mile.

Ironically, she thought of the day they'd gone to Pelican Point. They'd wandered a mile along the lakeshore and had found the dead body floating in the water.

Bill Schroeder. She hadn't known that at the time, but it still gave her the creeps to think about it now.

So much had happened since then. It seemed like weeks instead of days since Rafe had come back into her life.

"No, Mommy," Brianna protested. "Can't we walk for a little while longer? Please?"

Just then she heard the sounds of bells. Church bells.

In the distance, she could make out the peak of a church steeple in a break between the trees.

"All right, we'll walk a little while longer," she agreed. Brianna skipped with glee and Kayla hurried to catch up with her daughter and the ever curious Clyde. She couldn't deny a pang of curiosity that made her want to follow the pretty sound of the church bells and to catch a glimpse of the church.

What day was it? Tuesday? Were there church services on Tuesday mornings?

Maybe, if it was a special occasion.

The highway curved and as they rounded the bend, Kayla realized they'd gotten much closer to the town of Willow Grove than she'd realized. And there, off to the left was a small church, nestled in a small clearing surrounded by trees.

There was a parking lot off to the right, and she was surprised to see there were at least two dozen cars parked there. As they came closer, she realized there were people walking into the church.

Did the bells signal the start of the service? Was this a regular service or something special? She wasn't sure but she had an overwhelming urge to find out.

"Bree, tie Clyde to that tree there, would you?" Kayla asked. "I want to go inside for a few minutes."

"Okay." Apparently, Brianna was agreeable to anything that didn't require her to turn around to head back to the motel.

Her curiosity was stronger than the feeling of acute self-consciousness as Kayla held Brianna's hand and walked into the church. Beautiful stained glass windows lined the walls, and there was a cross hanging in the front of the church. There weren't that many people seated in the pews, and she slid into the back, concerned that maybe this was either a wedding or a funeral service.

When the pastor came out, she quickly discovered the people were gathered for a funeral. She was about to leave when she felt the pastor's gaze on her. Flushing, she bowed her head, feeling like an interloper.

But as the pastor spoke, she discovered the simple funeral service was for a member of the congregation who was elderly and didn't have any family left. Those who'd attended may have only known the gentleman in passing.

Brianna didn't seem to mind sitting there and listening, so they stayed.

Being in church made Kayla feel closer to God. She listened as the pastor spoke about the deceased, John Cornwall. She was struck by how the pastor believed John was in a much better place, now that he'd gone home to live with God.

Was this what Rafe meant when he said his faith had gotten him through his loss? He must believe what the pastor was saying as well. She'd honestly never thought of heaven very much. She'd been too focused on what she thought Jeremy was missing in life here and now. The fact he'd never see Brianna's solo in the school choir, wouldn't see her go off to her first day of high school, drive a car, graduate from high school and then college. Get married. Have a family of her own someday.

All the things she wanted to share with him. Had she been selfish to want Jeremy to stay, when—if she were to believe the pastor—he was in a much better place in heaven?

The service was brief, ending after twenty minutes. Kayla stood and waved to Brianna to follow, intending to slip out before anyone noticed.

"Who was that man who died, Mommy?" Brianna asked as they walked outside. "Was it the man who fell into the lake like Daddy?"

"No, sweetheart, he was a man who attended church here." It struck her that Brianna only mentioned her father because they'd sat through a funeral service. Was that always going to be how she remembered her father? And if so, maybe that wasn't such a bad thing.

"Okay." Brianna didn't seem too concerned one way or the other. She took off, eagerly heading over to the tree where they'd left Clyde.

"Ma'am?"

Kayla paused and turned around with a flash of guilt as she realized the pastor was talking to her. Was she in trouble because she'd crashed the funeral service? "Yes?"

"I wanted to introduce myself," he said, hurrying over. "I'm Pastor Thomas. Welcome to Saint Catherine's Church."

"Oh, ah, thanks. I—we were just passing through. I heard the church bells," Kayla explained, feeling exposed as a fraud. "I know I'm not a member of your church, but I enjoyed your service."

"Everyone who crosses the threshold is a member," Pastor Thomas corrected cheerfully. "I'm glad you came and you're certainly welcome back anytime. Our regular service is on Sunday morning at ten o'clock. I hope you can make it."

The thought of returning for church services was very appealing. What would Rafe think of the small church? Would he attend with them? She found herself hoping he would. "Maybe I will," she responded slowly. "Thanks."

"We're always thrilled to have new members," the pastor said with a smile.

"I'm just visiting the area," Kayla felt compelled to explain. "I don't live here."

"That's all right—visitors are always welcome, too."

He was just so nice and earnest she had to grin. "All right then, maybe we will come back on Sunday. It was nice meeting you, Pastor Thomas."

"Likewise," he murmured. "Have a good day, ma'am."

It wasn't until she turned away that she realized she hadn't offered her own name. Very rude.

She glanced over toward the tree where Brianna had tied Clyde, but she didn't see the dog or Brianna. With a frown of annoyance, she quickened her pace. "Brianna? Where are you? Wait up." Her daughter knew better than to take off on her own.

Certain she'd find Brianna and Clyde when she reached the road, she was surprised when there wasn't any sign of them. Where would they go? Had Clyde dragged Brianna into the brush in search of a squirrel?

"Brianna?" she called in a sharp tone. "Where are you?"

No answer. Not even Clyde barking. Brianna might try to hide as a game, but Clyde normally responded to the sound of her voice.

A cold sense of dread overwhelmed her. Where were they?

"Brianna?" Kayla pushed aside the churning nausea, as she desperately searched everywhere for any sign of her daughter. She hurried down the road in the direction from where they'd come from. There was a rustling in the bushes on the other side of the culvert and she glanced over, her gaze narrowing. Was Brianna playing a trick on her by hiding in the woods? If so it wasn't the least bit funny.

"Brianna, come out here right this minute," Kayla said in her sternest voice as she walked directly into the brush, swiping branches out of her face with an impatient hand. From the corner of her eye she saw something, and she started to turn. But she was hit hard on the back of her head.

Blinding pain exploded in her head, and despite her fear, she couldn't fight the darkness enveloping her.

TWELVE

Kayla moaned, blinking at the sunlight that pierced the back of her eyelids. Her head throbbed painfully, but she shoved the pain aside and dragged herself upright, glancing around in concern.

Brianna? Where was her daughter?

The area appeared to be deserted. She remembered seeing something in the bushes, but there wasn't anyone here now. Someone had been hiding here. Had he hit her over the head in order to take Brianna and Clyde?

Panic gripped her by the throat and she fumbled for her cell phone. She needed to call Rafe. And the police.

She reached into her coat pocket and pulled out a small cell phone wrapped with paper. She stared in horror at the object in her hand. Not her phone. Someone else's.

With trembling fingers she tore the rubber band from around the phone and read the note.

Don't call the police or we'll hurt the child and the dog. Wait for our instructions.

For a moment she stared at the block printing on the note, hardly able to believe what she was seeing.

They'd taken Brianna? Wait for instructions? What kind of instructions?

Where was her daughter?

Instantly, she turned her eyes heavenward. *Dear Lord, please keep her safe. I'm begging You, Lord. Please keep Brianna and Clyde safe in Your care.*

Kayla stifled a sob and scrambled through the brush and up through the culvert to get back on the road. The movement made her head pound, but she ignored the pain. Stuffing the foreign phone and note back in her coat pocket, she pulled out her own phone. Tears kept streaming down her face, blurring her vision, but she brushed them away so she could see as she dialed Rafe's number. She jogged down the highway, back toward the motel as she waited for him to respond.

"Hi, Kayla," he said by way of greeting.

"Rafe?" she couldn't hide her voice, thick with tears. "I need you. Brianna's gone. They've taken Brianna and Clyde."

"What?" Rafe flinched at the sound of Kayla sobbing in his ear. His plan of telling her what he'd found in Jeremy's memorial evaporated at the news. "What do you mean they've taken Brianna and Clyde? What happened? Where are you?"

"We took a walk, not very far, and we saw a church." He could barely understand Kayla's explanation through her choked sobs. He was already in his jeep so he quickly turned the key and slammed the jeep in gear. He stomped on the accelerator hard enough to make his tires squeal in protest. "We sat inside for a bit and then afterward the pastor wanted to talk to me. Brianna went to get Clyde and suddenly they were gone. When I was looking for her, someone hit me over the head and left me a note and a phone. I'm not supposed to call the police or they'll hurt her."

Kayla broke down then, sobbing as if her heart was being ripped from her chest. He could only grip the phone helplessly. "Kayla, don't. Please. I'll be there in a few minutes, okay? Don't go anywhere. Just stay there and wait for me."

He couldn't be sure she even heard him through her tears. He continued to repeat his instructions until she finally calmed down.

"Okay, but hurry." Her voice broke again. "Please hurry."

"I will," he promised his own voice thick with fear. As much as he wanted to keep Kayla on the line, he could drive faster if he wasn't talking on the phone. He snapped the phone shut and pushed the jeep as fast as he dared.

As he drove, his mind tumbled with questions. Why kidnap Brianna and Clyde? Because of the evidence they'd found in Kayla's house? The photographs? How had Landrum or whoever had killed Schroeder found Kayla at the motel? Rafe made certain they hadn't been followed. And he hadn't mentioned the location to anyone other than his commanding officer, Luke Sanders.

He trusted his commanding officer with his life.

But had Luke talked to Evan? The hairs on the back of his neck lifted as a chill snaked down his back. Of course he had. Luke had mentioned how he'd updated Evan last night on the latest turn of events. Luke wouldn't have thought anything about mentioning the name of the hotel where Rafe had taken Kayla and Brianna after the fire.

As much as he didn't want to believe Evan was guilty,

he couldn't ignore the possibility. Especially now that Brianna and Clyde had been kidnapped.

Who else would have known where to find them?

Feeling sick to his stomach, he pulled into the driveway of the motel. He grabbed the notebook he'd found in Jeremy's memorial and headed toward Kayla's door. She opened it up as if she'd been sitting with her face pressed to the window watching for him.

"Rafe," she sobbed, throwing herself into his arms. "They took her. They took my baby!"

"Shh, it's okay," he said, crushing her close as he half dragged her inside the motel room, kicking the door closed behind them. "We're going to find her, Kayla."

For a moment she simply sobbed against his shoulder, but then she seemed to pull herself together with a monumental effort. "Okay, what do we do first? Call the police? Or the FBI? Or do we need your boss to call them for us?"

He wasn't ready to call his boss, not yet. He put his hands on Kayla's shoulders and stared intently into her eyes, willing her to focus. "Kayla, I need you to trust me, okay? Show me the note and the phone."

She pulled the cell phone and the crumpled note out of her pocket and thrust them into his hands. Rafe took the items, searching for any potential clues.

"This is one of those throwaway phones," he murmured, turning the instrument over in his hand. The note didn't reveal much either. He set them aside and picked up the notebook, handing it to Kayla.

"Here's what I found tucked inside your husband's memorial down at Pelican Point," he said. "More evidence hidden by Schroeder. Names and dates and new identities of the criminals they've helped to escape."

Kayla's eyes widened as she took the notebook and

flipped through a few of the pages. "Why would he hide this in there?" Kayla asked in bewilderment. "I don't understand. Do you think Bill was looking for a way out? Was he intending to eventually turn this notebook and the photographs over to the police?"

"Maybe," he allowed. "But what's important is that we have it now. And Kayla, before we talk to anyone else, we're going to talk to Charlie Turkow."

"Charlie?" She stared blankly at him. "Why? I don't understand. We have to hurry. They took Brianna!" Her voice rose in panic.

"I know, and believe me, finding Brianna is my first and only priority." He surprised himself by realizing he'd spoken the truth. He would do whatever necessary to get Brianna back. Solving this case had become secondary.

Brianna truly was his one and only priority.

"So what are we waiting for?" Kayla demanded in an agonized tone.

"We can't just rush off without a plan," he told her, tightening his fingers on her arms. "Hear me out. We're going to find Charlie Turkow first. He seems to think that someone in the coast guard is working for Landrum. And I'm not calling my boss or anyone else in authority until we find out exactly who he believes murdered Schroeder. I need to know who he saw."

For a moment she just stared at him, but then she nodded. "All right, but let's hurry, okay?"

"Absolutely." Rafe was glad to see Kayla was willing to trust him. And he prayed he was worthy of her trust.

Heavenly Father, please show me the way. Give me Your strength and wisdom to find Brianna. Please keep Brianna safe in Your care, Amen.

* * *

Kayla sat in the passenger seat of Rafe's truck with Schroeder's notebook in her lap and the disposable phone clutched in a tight grip.

Inwardly she was screaming at Rafe to hurry. Everything around her seemed to be going in slow motion. She found herself pushing her right foot on the floor of the jeep, as if she could control the speed of the car through will alone.

Brianna. Sweet, innocent, Brianna. She needed to find her daughter.

She couldn't even consider the fact that Brianna might be hurt. Or worse.

No, she had to believe the kidnappers would keep her daughter alive. A dead hostage wouldn't help them.

She was glad, fiercely glad, they'd taken Clyde with them. At least Brianna wasn't completely alone.

Clyde wasn't exactly a guard dog, but he was loyal. He'd stay with Brianna.

"Are you okay?" Rafe asked, reaching over to put his hand on her knee.

Slowly she shook her head, a tear escaping from the corner of her eye to roll down her cheek. "We need to find Brianna, Rafe. How is talking to Charlie going to help?"

He glanced at her, his dark eyes intense with concern. "Trust me, Kayla. We'll find her. Why don't you look through Schroeder's notebook? We suspect there is some sort of drop-off location, where they pick up new identities for the criminals who are being smuggled out of the country. Maybe Schroeder has put something in the notebook about it."

She sniffled loudly and rubbed the tears from her eyes. "Okay."

Before she could even open the cover of the notebook, though, the disposable phone rang.

She froze staring at the instrument like it was a poisonous snake that might bite her. In a panic, she stared up at Rafe.

"Answer it," he directed her. "And don't mention me. Pretend you're alone."

She took a deep breath, opened the phone and put it next to her ear. "Brianna?"

"Your daughter is safe in our care," a mechanically distorted voice said in her ear. "And she will stay safe if you listen carefully and follow our instructions."

Anger flowed through her veins. "I want to talk to Brianna. I want to know she's unharmed."

"Do you have the evidence?" the mechanical voice asked, as if she hadn't spoken. "Answer yes or no. Do you have the evidence?"

"Yes," she snapped. Was this some sort of weird recording? Or was she actually speaking to a person? She honestly couldn't tell. "I have photographs and the notebook."

She wanted to hear Brianna's voice. She desperately needed to know her daughter was all right.

"Good. Listen carefully. You will call and make arrangements to obtain a rental car. You will leave the motel without talking to anyone. You will meet a man in a blue uniform at the corner of Dover and Barley in Green Bay in exactly six hours. You will come alone."

"And you'll bring Brianna?" she asked.

"Once we have the evidence, you will get directions to the location where we are keeping your daughter."

She saw Rafe shaking his head—the mechanical voice was speaking loud enough that he could overhear.

"No. Bring my daughter to the drop-off point, or I'm not giving you the evidence. I want to see Brianna."

"Six hours. If you're not there, we'll kill her." The phone went dead.

Kayla's fingers went numb and the phone fell into her lap. There was a loud roaring in her ears.

This couldn't be happening. They were stringing her along. Whoever had taken her daughter was going to kill Brianna and Clyde. They wanted the evidence, but somehow she knew that no matter what she did they were going to kill Brianna.

She burst into tears.

Kayla's shuddering sobs were like knife wounds to his heart. He reached over to take her hand, keeping his attention on the highway with an effort. He was torn between pulling over to comfort Kayla and the need to get to Charlie as quickly as possible.

"Kayla, please don't cry. We'll find her." He couldn't make rash promises, but he felt certain he was on the right track. He intended to verify with Charlie that Evan was involved, and if so, he'd take that straight to his commanding officer. With Luke's support they'd come up with a plan, mobilizing an entire fleet if needed in order to find Brianna.

None of which was going to make Kayla feel any better at this moment in time. He remembered all too well how awful it was to hold his wife in his arms, knowing she was bleeding to death and helpless to prevent it.

He glanced over at her, tightening his grip on her knee. "Kayla, listen to me. You're not alone. Brianna isn't alone. God is watching over her. Put your faith in God."

Kayla's shoulders were shaking, but after a few minutes, she managed to pull herself together. She swiped at her tears and sniffled loudly. "I know you're right. It's just so hard…."

"I know, but instead of imagining the worst, put your efforts into prayer." Although he'd prayed to God that snowy night five years ago, Angela along with Josué had still died. He'd tried to understand why God had called his wife and baby home without him, but deep down, he'd railed against the wisdom of God's plan. Still, his faith helped him through the darkest days. Knowing Angela and his son were in heaven next to God had sustained him.

"Okay," she whispered, squeezing his hand and then letting go. "I just wish I knew where they'd taken her."

"Read through Schroeder's notes," he suggested, knowing that having something productive to do would help. "Maybe there's something in the notebook that will help."

Instantly, Kayla straightened in her seat, her tears evaporating. She opened the notebook and began pouring through the pages.

He glanced at the clock, estimating they'd be at the lakefront within ten minutes. Once he knew for sure Evan either was or wasn't involved, they'd head straight for the substation and Luke. There wasn't a second to waste.

He pushed the accelerator harder, edging well over the speed limit. Why had the kidnappers given Kayla six hours to get to Green Bay? The situation didn't make logical sense. Unless they had to bring Brianna in from somewhere else?

But they hadn't agreed to bring Brianna to the drop-off point.

So that meant the kidnappers were someplace else. Somewhere far enough away that they needed time—six hours—to get to Green Bay.

Because they're out on the water? At the drop-off point?

If so, it was lousy planning on their part.

Rafe pulled into the Pelican Point parking area. Charlie's boat was moored at the dock, thankfully. Kayla clutched the notebook to her chest as they hurried down the pier.

"Charlie?" Rafe shouted as he jumped from the dock into the stern of the boat. "If you don't come out, I'm coming down."

"I told you to leave me alone!" The old man came up from below deck, holding a baseball bat in his hand and staring with undisguised hostility.

"You told me to look in the mirror," Rafe reminded him. "I did. I understand now that someone from inside the coast guard might be involved. But that's not important now. What is important is that whoever killed Schroeder has kidnapped a five-year-old girl."

"My daughter," Kayla added in a trembling voice.

Charlie looked at Kayla's tear-stained face and grunted something that might have been an acknowledgment or an apology. "So? What more do you want from me?"

Rafe reached into his wallet and pulled out a photograph of Evan that he'd taken on the first day he'd met the man. "I need to know if this is the guy who killed Schroeder?"

Charlie squinted at the photograph and slowly shook

his head. "No. The coastie I've seen is always driving that big ole fancy boat of his."

"Yancy?" Rafe stared at Charlie in shock. "Are you telling me the man in the expensive yacht is someone within the coast guard?"

"I've seen him wearing the uniform," Charlie confirmed. "But his name ain't Yancy."

He already knew they were using fake names. So maybe Yancy was former coast guard? That would explain a lot, considering the coast guard didn't pay well enough for a crew member to afford a yacht the size of Yancy's.

"So Yancy, or whatever his real name is, might be a former member of the coast guard. Or he still has connections within the coast guard. And he must be getting his money from the criminal relocation business." Rafe pulled out Kayla's sketch of Landrum. "But this isn't Yancy?"

"Nope. I've seen that guy with Schroeder once or twice, but he's not the coastie," Charlie grudgingly admitted.

Rafe was somewhat relieved to know Evan wasn't involved. He still wasn't sure how Kayla's location had been found, but it was possible Yancy had coast guard connections. "Thanks, that's exactly what I needed to know." He glanced over at Kayla. "Come on, we need to find my boss."

"We only have five and a half hours," Kayla murmured, glancing anxiously at her watch.

"I know. We'll have a plan soon, I promise." He helped Kayla off Charlie's boat and they made their way back to his jeep. Thankfully, the ride to the substation in Green Bay wasn't far.

Kayla continued poring over the notebook. "Rafe? I think I found something."

"What?" He pulled into the parking lot and glanced over. His eyes widened in surprise. "Is that a map?"

She nodded. "The map is of Lake Heron at the point where it connects to Lake Michigan. He describes a small island, off the Canadian coast, not far from the Manitoulin Islands."

Rafe's pulse kicked up a notch. "Let me see," he said, drawing the notebook out of her hands. Sure enough, Kayla found the location of the drop-off point. A thrill of anticipation shot through him. This was the hand-off spot, the place where the smuggled criminals were taken to get their new identities.

In his estimation, the island was a hundred and fifty nautical miles from Green Bay. Nearly five hours by boat. Leaving plenty of time to dock and then get to the drop-off point on Dover and Barley in Green Bay.

"Good work, Kayla. I think this is exactly where they're holding Brianna and Clyde."

THIRTEEN

Brianna was on the island. Somehow, the knowledge gave Kayla a thrill of hope. They'd get her back. Surely, they'd get Brianna back safe and sound. Kayla stared at the speck on the map, trying to imagine her daughter right now, curled up with Clyde who'd protect her, as she half listened to Rafe reporting the conversation they'd just had with Charlie to his boss.

"So Evan likely isn't involved," Luke murmured. "That's good."

"Yes, sir. However, we don't really know if anyone else from within the coast guard might be working against us, so I'd rather not use normal communication channels."

"I don't like it," Luke muttered darkly. He let out a heavy sigh. "I don't want to believe any of our men are involved, but I understand your concern. I don't have a good explanation for how they found Kayla's motel. Seems unlikely they could have found her location without inside information."

"It's possible Yancy managed to convince someone he was part of the crew," Rafe pointed out. "Someone to be trusted."

"Maybe. But it's not like we've broadcasted every

move over the radio, either. Only a handful of key people knew that detail. Which means our insider would have to be someone in a trusted position."

"Well, if Yancy was once in the coast guard, there's no telling who he'd convinced to turn against us."

"Maybe. Wait a minute." Luke frowned and began flipping through a stack of papers. "I have it here, somewhere. Here it is," he said, pulling out a single sheet of paper. "Recent dishonorable discharges. I asked for this report the other day, after Charlie told us to look in the mirror. I wondered if our suspect might have been once on the inside."

"Only five from the Pacific area and two from the Atlantic area in the last eighteen months," Rafe said, scanning the brief list from the two main divisions in the coast guard. He turned to the closest computer, dropped into a chair and began hitting keys on the keyboard. "I'll do a quick search on these guys, starting with the two from the Atlantic Area. I'm sure one of them must be Yancy."

"I've been trying to reach Evan, but no luck." Luke walked over to the radio system off to the side. "It's not like him to be silent for this long."

Rafe glanced up at that. "How long?" he asked sharply.

Luke glanced at his watch. "Almost twenty-four hours. I'll try again."

Kayla wanted to scream with frustration. Why weren't they getting on a boat to drive straight to the island? She wanted to rescue Brianna. There wasn't a moment to waste. Every second counted.

"Why does it matter which one of them is Yancy?" Kayla asked, looking over Rafe's shoulder as he did his search, barely reining in her impatience. "The important thing is to find Brianna, right?"

Rafe glanced up at her, his expression full of compassion. "We're going to find her, Kayla. I'm sure she's on Eagle Island. But we need to know exactly who we're up against. There may be something in Yancy's background that will help us."

"Still no answer from Evan," Luke said a few minutes later. "I think we have to assume the worst. Either Evan has been captured or he's working against us."

Kayla swallowed hard, unable to ignore Luke's grim expression. If Yancy had hurt or killed Rafe's partner, then there was no telling what he was capable of doing to a young girl and a dog.

For a moment the room spun dizzily. She grabbed the back of Rafe's chair to steady herself.

"Are you all right?" Luke asked with concern.

She swallowed hard and nodded.

"I found him," Rafe said, his voice ringing with satisfaction. "I'm sure this is Yancy. I haven't seen him up close, but this has to be him."

"Let me see," Luke commanded, coming around to peer at the computer screen. "Yes, that's him. Evan sent me a photograph of Yancy yesterday morning. I haven't heard from him since."

"Yancy's real name is Kevin Yarborough and he was arrested on a charge of embezzlement," Rafe said, reading the details of the guy's dishonorable discharge. "He did his time and was released fourteen months ago. Actually, both men from the Atlantic Area were released about the same time. The other dishonorable discharge was a guy named Giles Lieland."

"Gregory Landrum," Kayla whispered, staring in

horror at the photograph that bloomed on the screen. "That's him. Gregory Landrum."

Rafe glanced up at her. "Your sketch was right on. We have them, Kayla. Now we know for certain we're dealing with two former Guardians."

"And maybe a few others," Luke warned. "We can't know for sure who else might be involved."

"Schroeder was involved, but they killed him. Since they're asking for the evidence in exchange for Brianna's life, they must have realized Schroeder was building a case against them. That he was going to the authorities."

"Makes sense," Luke agreed.

"Let's go." Rafe stood, looking as if he wanted to jump into action. "I'm sure they've stashed Brianna and Clyde on Eagle Island. With our cutter we should be able to get there in a few hours."

"All right," Luke agreed. "We'll go. But I'm going to request a small backup team, too."

"I'm coming with you," Kayla announced.

Luke frowned. "I don't think that's a good idea."

Kayla glanced helplessly at Rafe. "Please? I need to come with you. Brianna will be scared to death. I need to be there for her. Please?"

She held her breath, waiting for Rafe's response. He wouldn't be so cruel as to keep her away.

Would he?

Rafe hesitated, glancing at his commanding officer. It went against his better judgment to allow Kayla to come along, yet he couldn't refuse her request. Especially since there was a possessive part of him that didn't want to let her out of his sight. She'd be safer with him, rather than staying in Green Bay all alone. "I think she could be of some use when we do find the child and the dog, sir."

Luke scowled. "Doesn't matter, she's a civilian."

Rafe took a deep breath. "I can't just leave her here, sir. And what about the drop? If we don't meet the kidnappers' demand in Green Bay at the designated time, they'll know something is up. I don't want Kayla involved in the drop without me being there with her."

"Maybe you're right. We can't do this alone. I'll ask the local authorities to take over the Green Bay meeting," Luke agreed thoughtfully. He reached for the phone. "I'm sure they have a police woman who can do the drop in Kayla's place."

"Might be better for the shore police to act as a backup to us as well," Rafe pointed out. "That way we wouldn't have to worry about a potential leak on the inside."

"All right," Luke agreed grudgingly. He glared at Kayla. "I don't like it. If you come along, you're doing so at your own risk."

"I know," Kayla said eagerly, determined not to be a burden. "I won't be a problem, I promise."

Rafe knew allowing Kayla to come along was totally against proper procedure, but the case had taken a strange twist with former Guardians involved. They couldn't even use their own crew for backup without knowing if any crewmen might have been compromised.

"I'll take full responsibility for her, sir," he said.

His boss raised a brow. "You'll stake your career on it?"

"Absolutely," he agreed, without the slightest hesitation. And he meant it.

Finding Brianna was his first priority. Nothing else mattered.

* * *

Kayla was relieved when Rafe's boss reluctantly allowed her to come along. There was a moment of panic when she wondered what would happen if they didn't find Brianna on the island but then she shoved the doubt aside. She trusted Rafe. And the island was the logical place for the kidnappers to have taken Brianna and Clyde.

Rafe insisted she take Dramamine to take to ward off potential motion sickness, and she didn't argue, unwilling to give him any reason to regret his decision. Now that they had a definitive plan, things moved quickly and within twenty minutes, they were on board the coast guard cutter, pulling away from the dock.

Luke ordered one of his most trusted petty officers to take control of the boat, but demanded radio silence. Petty Officer Phillip Durham looked at the commanding officer like he was crazy, but did as he was told.

She couldn't stay below in the cramped quarters. Up on deck, the wind whipped painfully around her.

The boat raced across the choppy lake water, heading due north. Despite the frigid air blowing across her face, Kayla stood at the rail, bundled in her coat her long scarf wrapped around her face, staring blindly out at the horizon waiting for Eagle Island to appear.

"Kayla, it's too cold to stand out here," Rafe murmured as he came up beside her. "Come down below. It's going to be a while before you can see anything."

She was freezing, but she couldn't drag herself away. She wanted to find Brianna alive and safe on the island so badly. And if her daughter had suffered physically or emotionally at the hands of her kidnappers, she wasn't sure how she'd cope.

In that moment, she realized she couldn't do this

alone. "I'm so scared," she admitted huskily. "Rafe, will you pray with me?"

"Of course I will." When he wrapped his arm securely around her shoulders and bowed his head so that it was close to hers, she leaned against him, gratefully. "Heavenly Father, please show us Your will. Give us Your strength and Your guidance as we face those with evil in their hearts. And please, Lord, keep Brianna safe in Your care. Amen."

Kayla hesitated a moment and then added her deepest fear, "And if you have chosen to bring Brianna home with You, please give me the strength to face whatever lies ahead. Amen."

"Amen," Rafe echoed in a low, husky voice.

In that moment a sense of calm flowed over her. It was like nothing she'd ever experienced before. Suddenly she wasn't afraid.

Because she wasn't alone.

God was with her.

This must be what Rafe had meant when he said he wouldn't have survived the loss of his wife and baby without his faith. This what she'd been missing in her life all along, what she'd been unconsciously searching for over the years since Jeremy's death. She tightened her grip on Rafe. "Thank you," she murmured.

"For what?" he asked in surprise.

She lifted her head to gaze up into his eyes. "For showing me how wonderful life with God can be. I wasn't happy, but hadn't realized what I was missing, until you showed me the way."

"Ah, Kayla. Your faith humbles me." He stared down at her for a moment and she waited breathlessly as he slowly lowered his mouth to hers.

His kiss was warm and tender. She reveled in the

sensation, feeling the effects of his embrace all the way to the depths of her heart and soul.

When he lifted his head, she buried her face against his chest, staggered by the abrupt realization.

She loved him. Loved Chief Petty Officer Rafe DeSilva with a depth that had been missing in her marriage with Jeremy. Not that she hadn't loved her husband, because she had, but this closeness with Rafe was so different.

Because they were also bound together by their love of God.

With God's help, they would find Brianna. She couldn't allow herself to consider the alternative.

Rafe stared down at Kayla, more shaken than he cared to admit by the impact of their kiss. He couldn't be in love with her. He wasn't ready for a family.

Brianna. Nothing mattered except finding Brianna. He needed to concentrate on saving Brianna, especially because it was his fault she'd been taken in the first place. He shouldn't have left them alone at the motel. In fact, he couldn't believe Kayla hadn't blamed him.

Instead, she'd kissed him as if she were drowning and he was a buoy.

He needed to focus on the danger that undoubtedly waited ahead.

He never should have agreed to have Kayla come along.

Somehow he managed to convince Kayla to go down below, out of the cold wind. His commanding officer had a topographical map of Eagle Island spread out on the small table in the galley. More than ready to get down to business, he took the seat across from his commanding officer.

"We're going to land on the island, here," Luke said, indicating a relatively small sandy area between two large rocky sections of shore.

Kayla leaned forward with a frown. "But isn't this beach area, here?" she asked, indicating the northeastern part of the island.

"Yes, and that's the spot the kidnappers are likely using for their access," Rafe explained. "We'll need to land where we're not expected."

"There isn't a whole lot of beach on this particular island," Luke said. "In fact, most of it seems to be covered in trees. I think this is the most logical area for a structure, up against the rocks. And if they have stashed Brianna and Clyde inside, I'm sure there will be men guarding them."

"I hope they're staying someplace with heat," Kayla murmured.

Rafe understood her concern. The weather has been mild for December, but a temperature in the high forties was still cold without a source of heat. "I'm sure they have a wood-burning stove or something. We know they're using the island as a staging place, an area to give the escaped criminals new identities and a place to stay for a while until the search dies down."

"They must have someone working with them from the Canadian border," Luke said. "Someone who can get into the Canadian ports easily."

"We'll find everyone involved, eventually," he said confidently. Many criminals were more than happy to rat out their pals. Especially if they thought cooperating would give them lighter sentences.

He and Luke planned out their approach. Kayla huddled beside him, listening wordlessly as they discussed strategy as they prepared for their approach. Once they had a plan, he and Luke double-checked their weapons and gear. He and Luke were armed but they needed to be certain Brianna didn't get caught in the crossfire.

And he wanted to give Kayla something to use to protect herself as well.

"Here's a flare gun," he said, lifting the small squat gun and handing it to Kayla. "Have you ever handled one of these before?"

"Never." She took it with an expression of distaste.

"I wouldn't point it directly at anyone because it will cause a severe burn, but if you need help, the flare gun will let us know you're in trouble."

"Okay." She took the gun, holding the business end downward.

"There's two flares, one on each side," Rafe explained, showing her the various aspects of the gun. "You just aim and shoot. They're actually pretty quiet. There will be a soft poof when you shoot it off, and then the orange flare will light up the sky."

"Sounds simple enough," Kayla murmured.

Rafe stared at her. None of this was simple. He was crazy to even consider leading Kayla into danger. But they were as prepared as they could possibly be.

All they could do now was wait. And pray.

By the time they reached Eagle Island sitting off the Canadian shore in Lake Huron, Kayla's nerves were stretched to the breaking point. Only through repeating her silent prayers was she able to maintain control.

Luke instructed the Petty Officer to moor the boat quite a ways off the island. They took a small rubber raft the rest of the way to the narrow part of the beach nestled between the two large rocks.

They all understood the plan so there was no need to talk. When they landed on the island, Luke pulled the rubber raft up out of the water, stashing it in a hollow between the rocks in case there were boat patrols. After dropping them in the water, the coast guard cutter had also backed away hiding in the distance. Once the cover of night had fallen, the officer had orders to come closer.

Rafe put a hand on her shoulder, indicating she should stay behind him as they crept silently through the trees, keeping behind the band of evergreens.

After roughly a hundred yards, Rafe paused and she came up beside him. He pointed through a gap in the branches and she sucked in a breath when she saw the log cabin about twenty yards away. There were two men standing guard outside the closed cabin door, each holding a rifle, speaking in low tones.

A barking whine reached her ears and she nearly wept in relief. They'd found Brianna and Clyde. Her baby was inside the cabin. So close.

She desperately wanted to go to her daughter.

Rafe glanced back at Luke and gave a short nod. She knew their plan was to create some sort of diversion to draw the guards away from the cabin doorway. What sounded so simple in the boat now seemed completely overwhelming. How could their plan possibly work?

The very distant sound of a boat motor made Rafe stiffen beside her. He shot a horrified glance at Luke, and his commanding officer immediately turned and headed back in the direction of the narrow beach to check the source of the boat.

Rafe gave her hand a squeeze and stayed where he was. After what seemed like forever, Luke returned, holding up the universal hand signal for "okay." Kayla could only assume the boat motor belonged to one of the boat patrols they'd feared.

Rafe nodded and Luke shot off the flare. The guards were too far away to hear the soft poofing sound, but when the light burst in the sky, the guards immediately broke off their low-pitched conversation.

"Stay and guard the bait," the heavier-set guy said as he broke away from the cabin, and came toward them. Hidden as they were between the branches of the trees, Rafe and Luke waited for him to get past, before they crept after them, moving silently, two Guardians against one kidnapper.

As much as she feared for Rafe's safety, she also couldn't tear her gaze from the cabin where she was certain her daughter was being held.

There was only one guard and now he paced nervously about six feet in front of the door. She clutched the flare gun in her sweaty palm and crept out around the tree. Pointing at a spot behind the remaining guard's head, angled away from the cabin, she shot off the flare.

When the light flashed in the sky, the guard instinctively took off in that direction, leaving the doorway to the cabin unprotected.

Kayla knew it was an impossible situation, but logic didn't matter. Every cell in her body demanded she protect her daughter. She'd willingly trade her life for Brianna's if necessary.

She ran, heading straight for the cabin door. Her heart thundered in her ears and her chest burned as she braced herself for the worst.

Capture. Or being shot.

She refused to let fear keep her from reaching her daughter.

Brianna, hang in there. I'm coming.

FOURTEEN

The interior of the cabin was dim but she quickly spotted Brianna lying on a cot in the farthest corner of the room. Clyde's leash was tied in a knot to the bedpost. When he saw her come in, he jumped up from the floor, barking like a fool, his whole body wagging in welcome as he recognized her.

She winced, knowing her attempt to sneak inside to get Brianna was obviously ruined, but she couldn't bring herself to care. Ignoring Clyde for the moment, Kayla flew to her daughter's side.

"Bree? Everything's fine. Mommy's here," she whispered, dropping the flare gun and stroking a hand over Brianna's tangled hair spread out over the bare mattress. But Brianna didn't move. Belatedly, she realized her daughter wasn't responding. Panic surged, choking her.

Was she too late? No, she forced herself to think rationally as Brianna's skin felt warm to the touch. She took a deep breath and gently felt for her daughter's pulse, hardly able to concentrate over the roaring in her ears as she feared the worst.

The reassuring beat of Brianna's heart finally made

its way through the internal terror and she relaxed, closing her eyes.

Thank You, Lord. Thank You for sparing Brianna's life.

She slumped against Brianna, burying her face against her daughter's hair for a moment before pulling herself upright. Okay, she needed to assess her options. The idea that Brianna had been drugged made her feel sick, but she took solace in noting how Brianna still wore the same clothes she was wearing earlier that day including her pink winter jacket, and appeared otherwise unharmed.

Maybe being drugged and oblivious to what was going on around her wasn't such a bad thing. She didn't want to consider how this entire event may have permanently traumatized her daughter.

She glanced around helplessly, feeling very alone without Rafe. She needed to get Brianna out of here. Now. There wasn't a moment to lose.

Please God, help me. Give me strength.

The door to the cabin flew open with a crash and she jumped around, her heart leaping into her throat. She swiftly scooped the flare gun off the bed, stuffing it beneath the waistband of her jeans in the small of her back, hoping her waist-length jacket was long enough to hide the weapon.

Ferociously, Kayla planted herself protectively between the armed man in the doorway and Brianna lying on the cot. The burly guard strode inside before slamming the door behind him. She couldn't help but flinch as the harsh sound reverberated through the room. She faced him bravely, grimly vowing he'd have to go through her in order to touch her daughter.

"Put your hands where I can see them," he ordered.

She noticed he was blinking rapidly as if partially blinded from light of the flare outside. "Don't move."

She lifted her hands—palms facing forward, trying to calm the raging beast before her. Surely he wasn't all bad. There had to be some humanity in him somewhere. "Please, I'm not armed. I only wanted to protect my daughter. Let her go," she begged. "It's me you want. I had the evidence, not her."

"Shut up!" he shouted. The way his gaze jerked around the room, she could tell he couldn't quite focus on her, maybe because her dark clothing helped her to blend into the surroundings. The cabin was pretty bare, a small table and two chairs in one corner near a wood-burning stove, and a small sink and counter along the other wall. She dragged her attention back to the man blocking her path.

"You can't escape," he growled as if sensing what she was thinking. "There's no way out."

Since she had no intention of going anywhere without Brianna, she ignored his threat. Still, fear was bitter on her tongue as she understood the gravity of her situation. Not that she regretted coming in to find Brianna, because she knew she'd do it again if necessary. But there was no denying her chances of escaping the man with a gun were very low.

Dear God, protect us. Guide me and give me strength.

Suddenly, she understood she needed to keep him talking. Rafe and Luke were out there and they'd already taken care of one guard. Surely they'd realize she was inside the cabin with Brianna. Between the two men they could handle this guy without a problem.

"You're friend isn't coming back," she said, striving for a matter of fact tone. "You might want to consider saving yourself. I'm sure the others aren't willing to risk their lives to come back for you."

"Shut up," he said again, but with less emphasis and she sensed her words had given him pause. He scowled at her and the slightest movement behind his head caught her eye and she held her breath as she realized the door behind him was slowly opening.

Another guard?

Or Rafe and Luke?

Please God, keep Rafe and Luke safe.

"Is the money they're paying you really worth dying for?" she asked, hoping to distract the guard from whoever was coming in behind him, praying the person was either Rafe or Luke coming to find her. "Because you need to know the island is surrounded by the coast guard. You can't win."

"Yeah, right," he sneered. "We're smarter than the coasties, any day. We found you stashed in that pathetic motel, didn't we?"

"Maybe. But how do you think I managed to find my daughter?" she asked logically. "Believe me, I didn't come alone."

For a moment he stared at her, and then his features twisted into a heavy scowl. "Why you little…" The guard took a menacing step forward and she eased back toward Brianna.

In that moment, the door opened and Rafe came in, lifting his arm high and smashing his gun on the back of the guard's head.

The guard let out a low groan and then collapsed, his big body hitting the floor with a solid thunk. She could only stare in shocked surprise, before gratitude flooded her.

Thank You, Lord. Thank You for protecting us.

Rafe quickly hauled the guard away from the doorway and used rope from his pack to bind the guard's arms and legs so he couldn't escape. When he finished, he glanced at her, faint accusation in his gaze.

"I can't believe you took off like that," he muttered grimly.

"I'm sorry," she whispered, knowing she deserved his anger. "I just had to come in to be with Brianna."

"You took ten years off my life," Rafe chided. But then he crossed over to embrace her in a huge hug that ended all too soon. "Brianna?" he asked, releasing her and kneeling beside the cot. "Is she okay?"

She swallowed hard and crouched beside him. "I'm pretty sure she's been drugged."

Rafe's jaw tightened as he gave a short nod. "Okay, I'll take her." Rafe lifted Brianna effortlessly into his arms. She wanted to protest, but knew he was stronger and could handle Brianna's limp weight far more easily than she could. "We have to get out of here. These two guards have been taken care of, but there are others, at least one for sure. Luke was watching the patrol boat but he should be here, soon. Can you carry the dog?"

"Yes, of course." Kayla bent over Clyde, yanking on the leash tied to the cot. It didn't give. For a moment she considered struggling to untie the knot, but then quickly unhooked his collar, freeing him. Without the collar she couldn't use rope as a leash so she gathered the cocker spaniel into her arms and followed Rafe outside.

As they left the cabin, a cautious hope filled her heart. They had rescued Brianna and Clyde from the two armed guards and helped even out the odds at the same time.

So far, so good.

With God's help and guidance, maybe they would be able to escape the island after all.

Rafe stayed close to the evergreen trees as he headed down the path back in the direction of where they'd left the boat, near the narrow opening along the rocky shore. The temperature had dropped several degrees as the sun slid behind the horizon. There was still some light to see, but he sensed it wouldn't last long. He moved as swiftly as he dared, every sense on heightened alert.

As glad as he was to have found Kayla and Brianna, he couldn't get rid of the nagging feeling that something was wrong. There were too many guards here on the island, especially since the kidnappers were planning to pick up the evidence in Green Bay. Was this a trap?

He'd left Luke near the coast and the rubber raft, so he could get a look at the man driving the patrol boat to make sure it wasn't Evan having gone over to the other side. Luke was supposed to come after him once that was done, and the patrol boat had already been approaching, so he'd expected Luke to meet up with him at the cabin. And if not at the cabin, along the path for sure.

But there was no sign of his commanding officer.

Had something happened?

They shouldn't have split up.

Clutching Brianna against his chest, he slowed his pace, listening hard for any indication that someone else might be approaching. Every nerve in his body jangled with warning. He could hear Kayla's breathing behind him as she struggled to move quietly yet quickly.

The nagging feeling wouldn't leave him alone. They were almost a hundred yards from the cabin when he came around a particularly large tree. He stopped abruptly in his tracks, causing Kayla to stumble against him.

Three men stood blocking the way just twenty feet in front of them.

His gut clenched as he saw how Giles Leiland and Kevin Yarborough both had guns pointed directly at him and Kayla. Unfortunately, a handcuffed Luke was also sandwiched between them.

"Don't move," Leiland warned as Rafe briefly considered his options. "No one, not even a Guardian, can outrun a bullet."

Rafe heard Kayla make a soft sound of distress, and he couldn't blame her. He didn't like the odds much himself. They were seriously outnumbered, now that Luke had been captured. He locked gazes with his commanding officer, and Luke's grim expression warned him that help might not be on the way. He couldn't tell by his boss's dark look if the man driving the patrol boat was Evan or not.

He didn't know what had happened, or how Luke had been captured but his heart sank to the pit of his stomach as he silently acknowledged there was a distinct possibility they may not get out of this alive.

Dear Lord, protect us from evil. Keep us safe in thy care.

He firmly believed the Lord was watching over them and took heart that they weren't beaten yet. Kayla came up to stand beside him and he scowled and shook his head. "Get behind me," he muttered.

"No," she said softly. He wanted to argue but at that moment, Clyde began barking furiously, struggling against Kayla's grip as if he were a huge guard dog instead of a friendly cocker spaniel.

"Shut that mutt up!" Leiland shouted, clearly uncomfortable with the dog's obvious aversion toward him. "I told that idiot guard to kill that thing."

"Easy, Clyde," Kayla said, tightening her grip on the dog, but Clyde ignored her. Rafe remembered Kayla once mentioning how Clyde didn't like her odd guest, Gregory Landrum. The way the dog continued to growl and bark at Leiland, he could see why Leiland was getting nervous.

"Drop your gun, DeSilva," Leiland ordered harshly. "Now."

Rafe didn't want to give up his weapon, but he didn't see any way around it, so he shifted Brianna in his grasp so he could toss the gun to the ground in front of him.

"Kick it toward me," Leiland commanded.

Rafe gave it a halfhearted kick, the gun landing still a few feet away from the two armed men. Leiland glanced at the dog and then over at Yarborough. "Get his gun," he said.

Yarborough came forward and picked up Rafe's gun, tucking the weapon into his coat pocket before going back to stand beside Luke.

"Give it up, Leiland. The game is over," Rafe said, injecting false confidence in his tone. "We have the island surrounded. You're not going to get away with this."

Leiland let out a harsh laugh, but his gaze kept going back to the dog, who continued to growl at him. "Nice bluff, DeSilva, but you're way off base. I knew you'd come out here and I'm willing to bet you have the evidence I want stashed on your boat. Once I get rid of Schroeder's stupid photographs and notes, not to mention killing each of you, there will be nothing to stop me."

Rafe helplessly glanced at Yarborough who seemed happy enough to defer to Leiland, waiting for orders.

"I'll give you the evidence," Rafe said, trying to reason with him. "Just let the woman and the child go."

"No deal. Slowly turn around and walk back toward the cabin," Leiland instructed. "If you try to run, I won't hesitate to shoot you in the back. At this point, I have nothing to lose and no reason to keep you alive."

Crushing a wave of helplessness, Rafe believed him. The only reason they were still alive now was because the evidence was stashed on the boat. He slowly turned to do as he'd been told. Desperately, he tried to think of a way out of this mess. Clearly, Luke hadn't had time to get in touch with the local police who were out on the water, waiting for them. There had to be a way to escape, at least long enough to make contact with the Green Bay police.

Kayla came up behind him, tugging on the back of his jacket. He slowed his pace, wondering if she needed help when he felt her tuck something hard into the center of his back. It took him a moment to figure out what she'd given him.

The flare gun! Not as good as a regular gun, but certainly better than having no weapon at all.

He turned to give her a thankful glance full of approval and she tried to smile, but the gesture didn't quite reach her eyes. The pain in her gaze as she stared at her daughter made him wish he'd listened to Luke and forced her to stay at the motel.

At least she would have been safe.

He couldn't stand the thought that his lack of planning might cause another innocent woman and child to die.

Lord, please guide me. Take my life if need be, but

spare theirs. Please Lord, protect Kayla and Brianna. They deserve to live.

Rafe felt a strange calmness cloak him after his reverent prayer. Kayla had given him the flare gun. Even with the weapon in his possession, he knew the odds were stacked against him.

But they also had God on their side. He knew that if he put his faith in God's hands, the Lord would save them.

Kayla stumbled over a tree root and almost fell. She stopped, trying to regain her balance without losing her grip on Clyde. Rafe turned, glancing back at her questioningly, silently asking if she was all right.

"Keep moving!" Leiland shouted from close behind them.

Clyde reacted instantly to the sound of Leiland's harsh command, barking loudly and struggling against Kayla's hold. During his struggles, his head butted sharply up against her chin, with a loud crack. She cried out in pain, loosening her grip.

That was all Clyde needed to break away. The dog hit the ground and took off straight for Giles Leiland.

"Get that dog away from me!" Leiland shouted, as he fired several wild shots, thankfully missing the dog.

This was the break he'd been waiting for. Rafe turned and thrust Brianna into Kayla's arms, not stopping even when Kayla almost fell to the ground in surprise, unprepared for the weight of her daughter's limp form.

"Get down!" Rafe yelled, making eye contact with Luke. Luke knew what he was silently asking and instantly dropped to the ground, making himself as small a target as possible.

Rafe held his breath and aimed the flare gun directly at Leiland, whose attention was torn between Rafe and the dog who'd latched onto his ankle with a fierce grip. *Dear Lord, forgive me,* he thought as he pulled the trigger, sending the heat of the flare at the man who he firmly believed intended to kill them.

"Noooo," Leiland howled as the full force of the flare hit him in the chest. His jacket burst into flames and he stumbled backward and fell, hitting the ground with an awkward thud, the gun in his hand going off one last time.

Time seemed to stand still as Leiland desperately rolled on the hard, cold ground, in a meager attempt to put out the fire. The man's agonized howls echoed horribly in the night.

Rafe forced himself to ignore Leiland. With one enemy down, he glanced over at Yarborough who'd thrown himself out of the way of the flare, but was now struggling to regain his balance, pointing his gun directly at Rafe even as he shot desperate glances to where Leiland lie motionless on the ground.

Rafe braced himself for the hit he knew was coming. Luke struggled to get up onto his feet, but with his handcuffed hands, there wouldn't be much his commanding officer could do to help. Rafe pointed the flare gun at Yarborough and squeezed the trigger, but nothing happened.

There were only two flares and they'd both been spent.

In that moment, hopelessness washed over him. There was nothing more he could do except to try and protect Kayla and Brianna.

"Get down," he shouted, pushing Kayla back into the heavy branches of the evergreen tree. He crouched in front of her, knowing his mere flesh and blood wouldn't be enough of a determent against a bullet.

Clyde yelped, backing away from Leiland, whose jacket was still smoldering as he lay inert. In the past few minutes, the man had stopped screaming and Rafe suspected Leiland was dying if he wasn't already dead. Clyde must have thought so, too, because he ignored Leiland to run in circles in front of Yarborough, barking like a mad dog, but didn't attack. Instead he tried to bite the second criminal, as he had Leiland.

Clyde was smart, but not that smart. He knew Leiland was an enemy but wasn't sure about Kevin Yarborough.

"Drop it," Yarborough said, eyeing the flare gun Rafe still clutched in his hand suspiciously. The fear in Yarborough's gaze convinced Rafe that the other man didn't know for sure if the second flare was present or not. The knowledge gave him a glimmer of hope.

"No. Give it up, Yarborough. It's over. Drop your weapon," he said sternly, bluffing with every bit of acting ability he possessed. When Kevin hesitated, he pushed a little more. "Go ahead, then. You might be able to shoot me, but I'll still get off a shot, too, and going up in flames isn't a pleasant way to die."

Clearly, the possibility of ending up like Leiland had given Yarborough reason to pause, especially with Leiland's body clear evidence of the horrific outcome. Yarborough stood uncertainly, obviously torn, especially, Rafe sensed, without anyone around to take charge of the situation, telling him what to do. Yarborough was a follower, not a leader.

No wonder he hadn't made it in the coast guard.

Rafe held his breath, hoping, praying there was a way out of this. He edged out toward Yarborough, advancing slowly.

"Stay back," Yarborough said again, but his tone wasn't nearly as convincing.

Rafe tensed when he heard a shout. What in the world?

Evan Marshall, his missing partner, burst up the path, his expression fiercely intent as he held a pointed gun.

Rafe froze, his heart thundering in his chest.

Was Evan there to help? Or had greed turned him to a life of crime?

FIFTEEN

"Drop your weapon," Evan said harshly. For a long second, Rafe honestly didn't know who his partner was talking to, him or Yarborough.

But when Yarborough spun around to face Evan in surprise, Evan leveled the gun at the crook. "I said drop it," he repeated in a warning tone. "Or I'll shoot."

Yarborough dropped his gun and then lifted his hands over his head in the universal gesture of surrender. Luke finally managed to find his footing and stepped forward to kick the gun well out of reach.

Rafe dropped his useless flare gun, his shoulders sagging with an overwhelming sense of relief. Thankfully, his fears over his young partner were unfounded. Evan wasn't one of the bad guys.

"Where have you been Marshall?" Luke demanded testily, staring at Evan in shock as his partner quickly tied Yarborough's arms behind his back. The annoyed question told Rafe that his commanding officer had resigned himself to believing Evan was either dead or working against them. "You haven't been in contact for over twenty-four hours."

Even in the dim light of the sun slipping behind the horizon, Rafe could see his partner flush, his jaw tight.

"They hit me on the head and tied me up and left me on Yancy's, or rather, Yarborough's yacht. It took me a while to get free. I overheard their kidnapping plan, though, and figured I needed to get here as soon as possible."

"Your timing was perfect," Rafe said, meeting Evan's gaze gratefully. "I'm not sure we could have gotten out of this without you. My flare gun was empty. We were trying to get by on a bluff and a prayer."

Evan flushed again and grimaced. "Thanks, but I blew it by getting caught," he acknowledged, owning up to his mistake. "I'm sorry, sir," he said to Luke, his expression full of chagrin. "But you'll be glad to know I did make radio contact with the crew and they're on their way." Evan looked as if he would do anything, including standing on his head and spinning like a top, in order to get back into his boss's good graces.

Rafe didn't want to mention how lucky Evan was that he hadn't been killed outright, suspecting Evan had already figured that out on his own. He couldn't help feeling a twinge of guilt at doubting his partner in the first place. Obviously, he owed Evan an apology.

"Since I'm standing here in cuffs, there's not much I can say. Help me out of these things," Luke said, lifting his bound wrists. "And we'll call it even."

A wide grin split Evan's face as he dug for a handcuff key. "Yes, sir!"

"A bluff?" Yarborough suddenly bellowed. "The flare gun was empty? I should have shot you."

Rafe raised a brow at their captive crook. "But you didn't."

"No, but I placed a tracer on your jeep," Yarborough said smugly. "That's how we tracked you to the motel."

Rafe's jaw tightened with anger. His jeep? That meant this was his fault. Brianna's kidnapping was his fault.

He heard a small sob and spun quickly, Yarborough forgotten. He stared down at Kayla sitting between the branches of the evergreen tree, cradling Brianna in her arms, silent tears streaking down her cheeks.

"What's wrong?" he asked in alarm as he went over to kneel beside her. "Are you hurt? Is Brianna hurt?"

Kayla shook her head and sniffed loudly. "Nothing's wrong," she managed in a shaky tone. "I'm happy. We almost died, but now we're safe. It's over. I can't believe it's really over."

"Yes," he murmured, pulling her into his arms, as close as he could with Brianna between them. "I'm so sorry, Kayla. You're safe now. It's finally over."

"We owe it to God for saving us," Kayla said, gazing up at him. His heart stumbled in his chest as he humbly realized he'd accomplished his original mission. Kayla had come through this experience with a renewed faith.

"You're right, we do." He took a deep breath and then spoke quietly, praying out loud. "Thank you, Lord, for giving us the strength and the courage to face and conquer our enemies. Thank you for keeping us safe in your care. Amen."

"Amen," Kayla echoed in a low voice.

Kayla could have stayed in Rafe's warm embrace forever, but of course they needed to get off the island, so when he pulled away, she reluctantly let him go.

"We need to get back to the boat before it's too dark to see," he murmured.

She forced a smile. "I know."

"Sir, you're wounded!" Evan exclaimed.

"What?" Rafe's head snapped up and he immediately crossed over to his commanding officer's side. "What do you mean wounded? When? What happened?"

Luke grimaced and reached down to gently explore the injury on his lower leg where the bottom of his uniform slacks were darkly soaked in blood. "I was hit by one of Leiland's wild shots, but I think it's only a flesh wound."

"We'll need to get you back to the boat," Rafe said thoughtfully as he crouched to examine the wound. "There's a first aid kit there."

"Use my scarf," Kayla offered. She unwound the long knitted fabric from around her neck and tossed it to Rafe. He took the scarf and bound it around Luke's lower leg, in hopes of slowing the bleeding.

"Can you walk?" Evan asked doubtfully.

"I'm fine," Luke snapped, as if determined to minimize his injury. "Let's get moving before anything else happens."

Kayla was happy to comply, more than ready to see the last of this island. As beautiful as it was, she couldn't ignore the violence that had taken place there.

She knelt and tried to lift Brianna off the ground, groaning a bit as the aftermath of her adrenaline rush made her muscles quiver like wet noodles. "Rafe? I need help, I can't lift Brianna."

"I'll get her," Rafe assured, striding over. His adrenaline must still be surging through his system as he effortlessly lifted Brianna in his strong arms. "You'll have to get Clyde, though."

The dog had calmed down now that the danger was over, and had come over to stand beside Kayla and Brianna. She reached for the spaniel, knowing she owed

Clyde a debt of gratitude for the part he played in helping them to fight against Leiland.

"You're going to get lots of doggy treats when we get back home," she promised, pressing a kiss on the top of his soft fur. "Every day for the rest of the year."

Clyde licked her cheek, making her laugh.

They were a ragged bunch as they slowly marched toward the narrow opening between the rocks where they'd left their rubber raft. Luke limped noticeably but stoically refused help. Rafe carried Brianna, leaving Evan to keep his gun trained on Yarborough's back during the trek.

It took a bit of maneuvering to get them all settled into the small rubber raft. Between Rafe and Evan rowing hard, they made it back to the coast guard boat in record time.

Safe on the boat, Rafe placed Brianna on the galley table, on top of a pile of life jacket cushions. Kayla set Clyde down and went over to help examine Luke's injury.

"It's in an awkward spot," Luke muttered darkly as she unwound her long scarf from his lower leg. "I can't get a good look at it."

There were lights mounted on the boat which helped her see the length of the wound. Luke had been right. There was a long ragged gash in his leg, but nothing worse. She did her best to wash the area with soap and water, and then used the antibiotic ointment and dressings in the first aid kit to cover the still oozing wound. "This will have to do until we can get you real medical help," she told him.

"It's fine," he said with a grunt. "Thanks."

Kayla finished binding his wound with gauze, and then taped the edges snugly. "Actually, I'm the one who needs to thank you, Luke. I'm sorry for not obeying your orders. And I hope you weren't captured because of me."

Rafe glanced up and came over to join the conversation. "So what did happen?" he asked Luke with a frown. "I thought for sure you'd be just minutes behind me."

Luke's mouth thinned with self-reproach. "It wasn't anyone's fault but mine. I made sure the guy in the patrol boat wasn't Evan or anyone else from my crew, but I wasn't expecting Yarborough and Leiland to come out from behind the trees on the path back to the cabin. The guards must have given a signal of distress or missed a check-in for them to figure out we breached the island. I walked right into their trap."

"The flares might have tipped our hand," Rafe murmured. "We knew that was a risk of creating a diversion."

Kayla knew her flare likely hadn't helped matters. "I'm sorry," she said again. "It's my fault. I just couldn't stand being away from my daughter for another minute."

Rafe reached out to gently squeeze her shoulder, reassuringly.

Luke stared at her for a long moment, before shaking his head. "I can't blame you, Kayla. If my daughter had been in there, I probably would have done the same thing. All that matters now is that we made it out of there safely."

"Amen," Rafe agreed.

Kayla smiled tremulously, grateful he wasn't angry with her. "Thank you for saving my daughter, sir."

"I think you managed to contribute," Rafe said dryly. "Giving me your flare gun was pure genius."

Her smile faltered as she remembered Leiland's horrible death. She didn't think she could ever look at a flare gun again. "Clyde deserves way more credit than me."

"He's a good guard dog," Luke agreed before levering himself to his feet and hobbling toward the small wheel house, taking over the controls from Evan. "I'll take over now. Let's finish cleaning up this mess," he said.

"Aye-aye, sir," Evan agreed enthusiastically.

Kayla went down into the small galley to Brianna. She huddled next to her daughter, relieved to note Brianna was finally beginning to stir. She had no idea how much medication they'd given her, and suspected the effects of the drug would linger for a while yet, but at least Brianna was showing signs of coming around. Clyde stayed right near Brianna's side, as if determined to be there when Brianna awoke.

She glanced up when Rafe came to sit beside her. "It's nothing short of a miracle that no one was badly hurt through all this," she murmured. "Other than Luke, we all made it out relatively unscathed."

"I know." Rafe took her hand in his and stared at their interwoven fingers for a long moment, before hesitantly meeting her gaze. "I need to know the truth, Kayla. Do you resent me for putting your daughter in danger?" he asked quietly.

She considered his question very seriously for a minute, before shaking her head. "No, Rafe, I don't resent you. At first, maybe, but deep down I knew Brianna's kidnapping wasn't your fault. Bill Schroeder was the one who made the decision to hide those photographs in my house. If he'd gotten out of the criminal activity earlier, or had simply taken the evidence to the police, none of this would have happened."

Rafe still looked troubled. "I wanted to let you know, there's no evidence Jeremy was involved," he said slowly. "From the dates and timelines in Schroeder's notebook, we know the criminal activity started right around your husband's death. I hate to say this, but there's a good chance Jeremy might have been murdered."

She swallowed hard at his words, knowing they might be true, but the usual despair that she normally felt when thinking about Jeremy seemed to have vanished. She missed him, but she didn't grieve for him the same way she had. "I know, but truthfully that doesn't matter one way or the other. Yarborough will go to jail, and that's what matters."

"You're taking the news better than I thought you would," Rafe admitted.

She tried to help him understand. "Finding God has helped me a lot, Rafe. At first when Jeremy was gone I was angry at him for leaving me when I needed him the most. Selfish on my part, but that's all I could think about. Now I've come to understand, he's in a much better place."

Rafe's smile was strained. "Yes, he is. Just like my family is as well. I know what you mean about being angry. Except I've been mad at myself for not planning ahead and for getting us caught in the snowstorm when Angela and our son Josué died."

Kayla felt tears gather in her eyes as she thought about Rafe's loss. Losing Jeremy had been awful but she didn't know if she'd have recovered if she'd lost Brianna. To think he'd gone on after losing his wife and son was staggering.

Her heart squeezed in her chest as she looked at him.

How could Rafe ever think she resented him? Her feelings were quite the opposite.

She was very much afraid she loved him.

And while the knowledge should have filled her with joy, being on the coast guard boat with him like this, surrounded by the evidence of his career, only reinforced what she already knew. Rafe's job would consist of his being gone for long stretches of time. Days and nights.

Leaving her and Brianna home alone.

Just like Jeremy had done.

And worse, he'd be in danger. More danger than Jeremy had ever faced. Not just from the weather, but from armed men. Crooks who wanted to kill him.

Despair filled her heart. How could she face life if she lost Rafe, too?

Very simply, she couldn't.

"Hey, what's wrong?" Rafe asked, squeezing her hand gently dragging her attention from her depressing thoughts.

She forced herself to meet his gaze. "Nothing," she whispered, although she was sure the truth was reflected in her eyes.

"Kayla, once you've had a chance to recover from all this, I'd like to see you again," Rafe said.

She bit her lip and looked away. "I don't know if that's a good idea," she whispered, even though her heart was aching.

"Why not?" Rafe asked, refusing to be put off. "I can't believe your feelings toward me have changed. Surely you can't deny there's something special between us."

She wanted to deny what he was saying, but she

couldn't lie. "I care about you, Rafe. But sometimes, caring about someone isn't enough."

There was a moment of silence. "What do you mean?" Rafe asked, his gaze perplexed. "I'm not sure I understand."

She took a deep breath and let it out, slowly. "I loved my husband, but over the months he was gone at sea, I began to resent him for being gone so much. Brianna's first severe asthma attack happened while Jeremy was out on the lake. I was left to deal with her being sick and in the hospital, all alone. I think I made our marriage worse, constantly harping on how much he was gone."

"I know how awful that must have been for you, Kayla, but surely now you realize that bad things can happen even when you're not alone. Those moments when Yarborough held his gun on me, I feared he would kill me, and then kill you and Brianna, too." His voice was rough, and she was surprised to realize the depth of his fear. "I should know, Kayla. My wife and son died in my arms. I was right there with them, but in the end, it didn't matter. God had called them home, but left me here on earth all alone."

She sucked in a harsh breath, trying to imagine how it had been for him to hold his dying wife and unborn child in his arms. "I didn't know you held them while they died," she murmured. "I'm so sorry, Rafe. I didn't know."

Rafe didn't speak for several minutes, as if needing time to pull himself together. "In the past five years since losing Angela and Josué, I've drifted along in my life, dedicating myself to my career. I've never looked twice at another woman. Until I met you. I'll respect your wishes if you truly don't want to see me, but I hope you'll reconsider." Rafe's dark gaze pinned hers intently.

"Because now I know God kept me on this earth not to suffer, but to find you, Kayla."

Stunned speechless, she could only stare at him.

"Think about it," he begged, slowly releasing her hand and rising to his feet. "Please, all I'm asking is that you take the time to think about it."

As he walked away, she knew she didn't have any choice but to think about what he'd said. His words continued to echo in her mind, until Brianna began to wake up.

Grateful for the distraction, she eagerly tended to her daughter.

"Mommy?" Brianna said, dragging her heavy eyelids open.

"I'm here, sweetie," she crooned, soothing Brianna's hair away from her face. "You're safe, Brianna. We're on our way home. Everything is going to be just fine."

Brianna wrinkled her brow. "What happened?"

"You were taken to a small cabin, but you weren't hurt," Kayla explained, choosing her words carefully. "Do you remember being at the church with me? When we left Clyde outside?"

For several long moments, Brianna still looked confused, but then slowly knowledge dawned. "Yes. The man was there, the one who stayed at our bed-and-breakfast. He had Clyde, but Clyde looked sick. I ran over but he put his hand over my mouth and I couldn't breathe. Then I must have fallen asleep."

Then he must have given her drugs to keep her out of it, and must have drugged the dog at first, too, but Kayla didn't want to tell Brianna too much. "Well you're all right now, Brianna. And Clyde is right here." She gave the dog a pat on the head and his tail wagged gratefully. "We're going home."

"Good. But I'm hungry," Brianna said, glancing around curiously. "And where's Mr. Rafe? Maybe he'll have dinner with us again."

Kayla tried to smile, but inside, her heart was heavy. If she refused to see Rafe again, Brianna would be hurt.

But what was the alternative?

Was she brave enough to open her heart to Rafe in spite of his career? In spite of the constant danger he faced?

Lord guide me, show me the way.

Walking away from Kayla was the hardest thing he'd done in a long time. But he sensed she needed time.

And he'd stupidly just promised to give it to her. He thought he heard murmured voices, indicating Brianna might have woken up, but he forced himself to leave them alone.

Brianna might be traumatized from her ordeal.

And he wasn't a part of their family.

The ache in his chest tightened painfully. He tried to ignore the hurt as he entered the small wheelhouse where Evan and Luke were talking.

"What's going on?" he asked. "Fill me in."

"The crew is making a sweep of the island," Evan said in satisfaction. "We're rounding up the rest of Leiland's hired thugs."

"Good," Rafe murmured, glad he didn't hear a note of envy in his partner's tone. Apparently, Evan finally understood that being in the midst of danger wasn't exactly fun and games. The young man had grown up significantly in the past few days. "Did they get the two guards we left tied up? There's one in the cabin and one tied to a tree in the woods."

"I think they have them both," Evan said. "I'm surprised the guy in the woods didn't give you away."

"We put duct tape over his mouth," Rafe admitted. He was glad they'd only had one death as they rounded up the rest of the criminal smuggling ring. They'd broken up the ring. Except for one piece of the process. "Too bad we never found the guy who did the fake identities."

"Uh, actually, that was probably Yarborough's job," Evan said with a frown. "When I was on his yacht I found several fake passports for him, with both names, Karl Yancy and Kevin Yarborough, along with several others, likely for the rest of his criminal cohorts. He also had a sophisticated computer set up complete with a mini-camera to take pictures. I hate to say it, but Yarborough's fake passports were pretty good."

"That would explain why he was out of his depth with the seedy part of the job, like capturing criminals," Rafe said slowly. "Although I'm surprised, considering he was once a former Guardian."

"Everyone reacts differently under stress," Luke pointed out.

That much was true. But both Leiland and Yarborough were black marks against a branch of the service he very much believed in. Shaking off the troublesome thoughts, he grinned. "So we have them all."

"Not all," Luke corrected with a dark frown. "There's still someone working on the Canadian border patrol. However, I'm sure we can convince one of these guys to turn on their accomplice without too much trouble."

Rafe didn't like the thought of any of them getting off with a potentially lighter sentence, although the ringleader of the criminals was clearly Leiland.

And his sentence wouldn't be lightened one bit.

Leiland's fate was in God's hands.

Just as his future with or without Kayla and Brianna was in God's hands.

SIXTEEN

Giving Kayla the time and space she needed wasn't going to be easy, Rafe grimly acknowledged as they docked in Green Bay. Every cell in his body protested the need to let her go.

For so long he'd refused to consider having a family. Had tried to keep his distance from Kayla because he'd been leery of opening up his heart again.

But somehow, his feelings for her had grown deep, in spite of his attempt to remain friends only.

There was no point in denying the truth. He loved her. Loved Brianna as if she were his flesh and blood daughter. He'd offer to adopt Brianna, if Kayla wouldn't mind, so they'd really be a complete family.

But Kayla didn't feel the same way about him. At least, not yet.

And he wasn't sure how to convince her to give him a chance. To give their love a chance.

He couldn't imagine his life without her.

"Rafe?" Kayla turned toward him as they prepared to disembark from the boat. "Is there any reason we couldn't go home? Back to my B and B?"

He forced a smile. "No, there's no reason you can't go home. The danger is over. I'd be happy to drive you back to the B and B. We can pick up the items we left at the motel another time."

"Thank you," she murmured, wrapping her arm around Brianna's shoulders and holding on to the rope he'd fashioned into a leash for Clyde. "After everything that's happened, all I want is to go home."

Her words cut deep. Her home. Without him. He tried not to think about his empty house, knowing it was best to give her time to recuperate from the series of events. Danger had a way of heightening feelings and once the danger was gone, those same feelings could easily fade away as well.

He knew what was in his heart. Knew that he loved Kayla with his heart and soul. But it was only fair to give Kayla the time she needed to understand her own feelings.

He didn't want to think he imagined the love in her eyes, the intensity of her kiss, but seeing as she hadn't even agreed to see him again, he couldn't discount the possibility.

On the way back to Kayla's bed-and-breakfast, he stopped at a fast-food restaurant to pick up something for them to eat for dinner. He wasn't exactly hungry, but noticed Brianna devoured her meal in record time.

Brianna seemed to have bounced back from being kidnapped and drugged, but he knew she'd been through a terrible ordeal. And even though Kayla claimed she didn't blame him for Brianna's kidnapping, he knew better. The fault was his.

He should have sent Kayla and Brianna to Arizona with Ellen. He should have given them into God's care, rather than thinking he could protect them better.

Hadn't he learned that lesson five years ago, with Angela and Josué?

Lord, please forgive me.

When he pulled up to Kayla's home, things looked the way they'd left them. The burnt Christmas tree was still lying in the clearing and he wondered if Kayla would mind if he brought over a new one. He hadn't forgotten his promise to fund the repairs to her house, either. The next day he'd need to write up his report for Luke, but maybe the day after?

Kayla punched in the code for the security system and then ushered Brianna and Clyde inside. The acrid odor of smoke lingered, but Kayla didn't seem to care. Belatedly, he remembered her room was still a disaster with its slashed mattress, but there was always the room Ellen had been using.

Kayla was strong. She didn't need him. Rafe stood awkwardly on the porch as she turned to face him.

"Thank you, Rafe. For everything," Kayla said, her expression serious.

He tried to smile. "I'm the one who should thank you. Please call me if you need anything."

There was a slight hesitation before she nodded and his stomach clenched when he realized she had no intention of calling.

"Goodbye, Rafe," she said, her voice so low he almost couldn't hear her.

Goodbye. Not good-night, but goodbye. He stood, his feet rooted to the floor. "Kayla, wait," he said as she started to close the door. He couldn't walk away. Not like this. "I'll give up my job at the coast guard. For you. For us," he amended. "Please give me another chance."

"You'd give up your job?" she echoed, her jaw dropping open in surprise. "But you love your work."

"I love you more." The words weren't nearly as

difficult to say as he'd anticipated. He wanted to haul her into his arms and to kiss her, but forced himself to take a step backward giving her the space he'd promised. "I'll call you in a few days," he said. "Just think about what I said, please?"

"I will," she agreed. And he found he was glad to have at least that small concession.

"Good night, Kayla." He turned and walked down toward his jeep, feeling her gaze on his back.

Lord, I know I don't deserve her so give me Your strength and guidance here. Show me Your will. Amen.

Kayla spent the next two days putting her house back in order and keeping a close eye on Brianna. She dragged the slashed mattress outside and put her room back together. The damage from the fire didn't look nearly as bad once she washed the walls. The drywall would need to be replaced, but otherwise the damage was minimal.

Brianna was quieter than normal but didn't seem to be too traumatized by the kidnapping. The hospital said Brianna was fine. She'd cried out in the middle of the night during a bad dream, but when Kayla gently probed to find what the dream was about, Brianna avoided talking about it by claiming she couldn't remember.

Kayla didn't push, knowing Brianna had to deal with what happened in her own way. But she prayed nightly for God to help her daughter heal without ill effects from the kidnapping and being drugged.

And she also prayed for direction as to what to do about her confused feelings for Rafe.

No matter what she did to keep busy, she couldn't get Rafe out of her mind. Dozens of times she'd been tempted to pick up the phone to call him. To share every bit of her life with him. He'd told her he loved her.

She wanted so badly to believe him.

But when she considered a future with Rafe, she couldn't envision how they'd make things work. She was humbled by his offer to give up his career for her. For them. But try as she might, she just couldn't imagine what Rafe would do if he wasn't part of the coast guard.

She'd fallen for the man in the uniform. The brave man who'd risked everything to protect her and Brianna. What right did she have to ask him to leave it all behind?

Very simply, she didn't.

Which meant, she had to figure out if she could live with the reality of his being gone and constantly in danger all the time.

The day before Christmas Eve, she was surprised by a knock at her door. When she opened it, there was a huge Christmas tree propped there.

When Rafe poked his head out around the branches, she couldn't help but smile. "Hi," he greeted her in a friendly tone. "I hope you don't mind that I brought you a replacement tree to take the place of the one that burned."

Since she'd been planning to go out that day to find one herself, she couldn't complain. "Impeccable timing," she said, opening the door wider. "We were going to head out today to get one for ourselves."

Rafe shoved the fir through the doorway, dropping hundreds of tiny needles on the floor as he carried it over to the corner of the great room where the old tree had been. "There wasn't much to pick from," he said apologetically. "I think this one is a bit lopsided."

"Lopsided is fine with us," she assured him.

"Mr. Rafe!" Brianna shouted, racing into the great room and throwing her arms around his legs in a hug. "You're back!"

Kayla's throat closed at the flash of longing in Rafe's eyes as he gazed down at Brianna. "I brought you a new tree and I have lights and ornaments in my car, too. Maybe you'll help decorate, *mi nina?*"

"Yay!" Brianna shouted. "Can I go outside to get the ornaments, Mommy? Please?"

"Of course," Kayla said lightly, although letting Brianna out of her sight still wasn't easy. Logically she knew the danger was past, but she couldn't help feeling anxious as Brianna darted outside to Rafe's car.

"Can you hold the tree stand steady?" Rafe asked, dragging her thoughts from her daughter.

"Sure." Kayla had rescued the old tree stand and had placed it in the corner ready for the new tree. She knelt on the floor, helping to guide the freshly cut stump of the tree into the stand, tightening the four screws to keep it sturdily in place.

"Perfect," Rafe said in satisfaction.

She couldn't help but agree.

With Brianna around, they didn't exactly have private time to talk, but Kayla couldn't help notice how nice it was to have Rafe there helping to decorate the tree.

She brought out a tray of hot chocolate and cookies, which Rafe seemed to appreciate as much as Brianna did. They took a few moments to enjoy the treat, gazing at the brightly decorated Christmas tree.

"I wanted to let you know that I've arranged for a new mattress to be delivered and for your drywall repairs," Rafe said, glancing at her over his steaming mug of chocolate. "But unfortunately, I couldn't get anyone to come until after the holidays."

"I have homeowner's insurance to pay for the damages," she reminded him. "But thanks. I wouldn't have had any idea who to even contact for help."

"No problem," he assured her. Rafe drained his mug of chocolate and set it aside before reaching for his jacket. The usual cold weather they normally had in December had blown in with the north wind. The weathermen were predicating snow for Christmas. "Well, I'd better get going. Take care, Kayla. Bye, *mi nina*," he added to Brianna, gently stroking her hair.

For a moment Kayla stared at him, blankly. He was leaving already?

Say something to make him stay.

Her mind went blank as he made his way toward the door. She hurried after him.

"Rafe?"

He paused in the act of opening the door, and then turned to face her. "Yes?"

"Ah, do you have plans for Christmas?" She winced at the blunt question that tumbled from her mouth and hastened to clarify, "I mean, would you be interested in coming for dinner on Christmas Eve? If you're not working, that is."

He stared at her for several long seconds before a tentative grin creased his face. "I'm not working and I would love to share dinner with you tomorrow."

There was so much more she wanted to say, but with Brianna standing right there, this wasn't the time or the place. Although she loved her daughter dearly, she wished reverently that she could have just a couple of hours alone with Rafe.

"Wonderful. Maybe stop by around five-thirty or

six?" She had no idea what she'd even serve, but that didn't matter.

She just needed to see him again. Soon.

He nodded. "See you at six, then," he murmured. His dark eyes lingered on hers intently and she felt breathless and tingly, all the way down to her toes.

She couldn't have looked away from him if her life depended on it. Thankfully, Rafe broke off the intangible connection shimmering between them by turning and walking back toward his car before she made a complete fool of herself.

"Mommy? It's cold," Brianna complained and she belatedly realized she was still standing there with the front door wide open.

"Sorry," she muttered, closing the door with a decisive click. As soon as Brianna was tucked in bed for the evening, though, she hurried to the kitchen, determined to plan Rafe a home-cooked meal he would never forget.

Rafe pulled into Kayla's driveway at exactly five minutes before six. He threw the gear shift into park and then turned the key in the ignition, swiping his sweaty palms on his jeans before reaching over to grab the two Christmas presents he'd brought.

For a moment doubt clouded his mind. Had he misinterpreted Kayla's invitation to be something more?

He'd spend the past few days in prayer, searching for guidance. And during that time, he'd realized he needed to let go of the past before he could move forward.

He could accept God had forgiven him. But he'd needed to learn to forgive himself. God's plan always superceded his own. Why it had taken him so long to figure that out, he had no idea.

Peace filled his heart and he could sense Angela was up in heaven looking down at him with approval.

He loved Kayla. And he was willing to do whatever necessary to show her that he would always be there for her.

No matter what.

Firming his resolve, he climbed out from behind the wheel and walked up to the doorway. Brianna opened the front door before he could even knock.

"Mr. Rafe!" she greeted him excitedly. "You brought presents!"

He couldn't wait until he'd earned the right to have her call him dad. With a grin, he handed over her gift. "This one is for you."

"I'll put it under the tree," Brianna said, gazing at the wrapped box in awe. He followed her to the tree, placing Kayla's gift beside Brianna's.

"Hi, Rafe," Kayla greeted him, coming out from the kitchen. He turned to look at her and his heart jumped into this throat when he saw her. She was breathtakingly beautiful. For a moment he couldn't breathe, her shiny mink-colored hair a stunning contrast to her Irish-green turtleneck sweater and pale skin. Her green eyes sparkled like emeralds. "Merry Christmas," she murmured, shyly.

"Merry Christmas," he returned, relaxing as he realized his instincts hadn't failed him. She'd asked him to come because she was considering giving him a chance. He walked toward her and took her hand in his, squeezing it gently. "Thanks for inviting me."

"I had to," she said, choosing her words carefully with a glance toward her daughter. "I couldn't bear not seeing you."

"Kayla," he murmured, reaching out to draw her close

in a brief, yet tight, hug. "I couldn't stand not being here."

Thankfully Brianna was oblivious to the undercurrent flowing between the adults as she chatted about how they'd spent most of the day cleaning up the various items of the Christmas village that had been covered with soot after the fire.

He tried to listen, but his gaze kept going back to Kayla. The meal she'd prepared was delicious, but he couldn't have told anyone what he'd eaten.

None of it was as important as being here with her, as part of the family.

"Can we open our presents tonight?" Brianna asked, once the dirty dishes had been cleared away and the leftovers stored in the fridge.

She'd directed her question to Rafe, and he glanced helplessly at Kayla. "Ah, I think that's up to your mother."

A small rueful smile played along her mouth. "Brianna, don't you think you should finish your surprise first?" she suggested evasively.

For a moment Brianna's eyes widened comically. "Oh, yeah! I almost forgot!" In an instant, Brianna turned and headed for her bedroom, closing the door behind her.

"Finally," Rafe muttered, crossing over to pull Kayla into his arms. "How much time do we have?" he asked, thankful when she wrapped her arms around his waist to return the embrace.

"Probably not more than ten to fifteen minutes," Kayla murmured dryly. "But I don't need much time to tell you how I feel, Rafe."

His heart hammered in his chest. "Kayla, there's no rush," he started to say, but she stopped him.

"Hush," she said, placing a finger over his mouth to prevent him from saying anything more. "I want you to know I love you. And I don't want you to give up your career for us."

Hope bloomed in his heart at her words. "Are you sure?" he asked hesitantly. "Because I don't mind finding something else to do, Kayla. I want you to be happy."

She smiled and reached up to press a quick kiss on his mouth. "I'm sure. I'm sorry I didn't tell you sooner, but once I really thought about it, I remembered how close I felt to God's presence when I went inside the cabin to find Brianna. I wasn't alone then, and I won't ever be alone now. And neither will you. I know there will be times you're in danger, but there are other careers just as dangerous. God will be with you, too. I love you, Rafe. And I want you to be happy."

"You've made me the happiest man on earth," he assured her, tightening his arms and crushing her against him. Now that he was holding her, he didn't want to let her go. "You've given me a family when I didn't even realize how much I wanted one."

"I'm glad," she whispered, pressing a kiss to his neck. He knew Brianna might come out any moment, but he couldn't help himself from kissing her again, desperately trying to show her with actions as well as words, how he felt.

The minute Brianna's door opened, they jumped guiltily apart, Kayla running a nervous hand through her hair.

"Okay, I have my present all finished. Can we open them now?" Brianna asked, skipping into the kitchen.

"Sure," Kayla said, but Rafe could tell she was flustered from the intensity of their kiss. She glanced at him, her eyes full of joy and longing. "Let's open our presents."

"Mine first," Brianna said when they were seated in front of the Christmas tree. She thrust a gift bag into his hands.

He opened the bag and drew out a picture that Brianna had drawn for him. It was a drawing of him wearing his dress blues and Brianna wearing her pink coat and matching hat. They were standing on the lakeshore, holding hands. His heart swelled with love. "It's beautiful, Brianna. Thank you very much."

"You're welcome." Brianna beamed at him. "Now it's Mommy's turn."

"Open yours first," he suggested.

Brianna didn't need to be asked twice. She ripped open her gift and gushed over the tiny miniature nativity scene. "I love it, Mr. Rafe."

He beamed. "I'm glad."

"Mommy's turn," Brianna said, keeping the nativity scene clutched in her hands as if she wouldn't let go.

He took the gift box he'd brought for Kayla and handed it to her. For several minutes, she simply stroked the smooth paper. "I don't have anything for you," she protested.

As if he cared. "A home-cooked meal was exactly what I wanted," he told her. "Go ahead and open it."

She bit her lip and then tore open the paper revealing a white box. She lifted the lid and carefully pulled out a church with a tall steeple, a poignant addition to her Christmas village.

"It's beautiful, Rafe," she murmured, her eyes bright with unshed tears. "I love it."

"I noticed you didn't have a church," he said. "Look inside," he urged.

With a slight frown, she gently opened the church door and peeked inside. He held his breath as she gazed in shock at the diamond ring.

"What's in there?" Brianna asked, moving closer. "A ring?"

"Will you marry me?" he asked.

"Yes!" Brianna shouted, jumping up and down with excitement. "Say yes, Mommy!"

Kayla smiled as she took the ring from inside the church. "Yes, Rafe," she said huskily. "Yes, I'll marry you."

"I've always wanted a new daddy," Brianna said, coming over to give him a hug.

He returned the hug and kissed the top of her head. "And I've always wanted a daughter like you," he said, as Kayla stood and came over to join them, his ring glittering on the third finger of her left hand.

He wrapped an arm around her, including her in the three-way embrace. He was glad Kayla had found God, and that she didn't want him to leave the coast guard, although nothing in the world was more important than what he had right here.

His family.

* * * * *

Dear Reader,

After introducing Kayla and Rafe in *Secret Agent Father*, I couldn't resist giving them their own story. Kayla's steadfast determination to keep her husband's memory alive for her daughter is admirable, but not if used as an excuse to stay in the past without moving forward with her future. Of course, Chief Petty Officer Rafe DeSilva won't let her get away with that for long, even though he has his own past to work through.

Living on the shore of Lake Michigan, I've always been intrigued by the skill and courage of the men and women who serve in the coast guard. Reading about one of their dramatic rescues gave me the kernel of an idea for this story. I'd like to mention a special thank-you to Lieutenant Ryan T. White for his assistance in helping me authenticate my story. Any mistakes are my own.

I hope you enjoy Kayla and Rafe's story, *The Christmas Rescue*. I always enjoy hearing from my readers and I can be reached through my website at www.laurascott-books.com.

Yours in faith,

Laura Scott

QUESTIONS FOR DISCUSSION

1. In the beginning of the story, Kayla is trying to keep her dead husband's memory alive for her daughter Brianna. Did you agree with this decision? Why or why not?

2. Early in the story Rafe arrives at the lakeshore to offer his assistance to Kayla and Brianna. Kayla is concerned because she doesn't want her daughter to become too attached to Rafe. Do you feel her concerns are valid, and if so, why?

3. Rafe has maintained his faith over the years despite the devastating loss of his wife and unborn child. Discuss a time when your faith was tested.

4. Rafe decides early on to keep his relationship with Kayla based on friendship and nothing more. How does his past loss influence his thoughts? And how has his faith suffered as a result?

5. Christmas is a special holiday. Discuss how both Kayla and Rafe managed to overcome their secret dread of the celebrations that normally take place during this time.

6. At one point in the story, Rafe tells Kayla the book of Psalms is his favorite. Discuss your favorite Bible verse and explain why it's your favorite.

7. Discuss Kayla's first exposure to church and how the pastor handled her presence there.

8. Kayla learns to pray when Brianna suffers her severe asthma attack after the fire. Describe a time when you realized the power of prayer.

9. One turning point for Kayla was when Brianna is kidnapped and she must lean on Rafe's expertise and emotional support. Discuss a time when an emotional crisis caused you to turn to God and to the person you love.

10. When Kayla and Rafe arrive on Eagle Island, Kayla sets off a flare and rushes in to find Brianna. Did she act appropriately or put them all at greater risk? Why or why not?

11. At what point in the story does Kayla fully support her faith in God? Discuss if you've ever had a similar experience.

12. How does Rafe convince Kayla of the true depth of his love? How did his faith impact this realization?

Love Inspired®
SUSPENSE

TITLES AVAILABLE NEXT MONTH

Available December 7, 2010

REQUEST YOUR FREE BOOKS!

2 FREE RIVETING INSPIRATIONAL NOVELS
PLUS 2 FREE MYSTERY GIFTS

Love Inspired®
SUSPENSE

YES! Please send me 2 FREE Love Inspired® Suspense novels and my 2 FREE mystery gifts (gifts are worth about $10). After receiving them, if I don't wish to receive any more books, I can return the shipping statement marked "cancel". If I don't cancel, I will receive 4 brand-new novels every month and be billed just $4.24 per book in the U.S. or $4.74 per book in Canada. That's a saving of 20% off the cover price. It's quite a bargain! Shipping and handling is just 50¢ per book.* I understand that accepting the 2 free books and gifts places me under no obligation to buy anything. I can always return a shipment and cancel at any time. Even if I never buy another book, the two free books and gifts are mine to keep forever.

123/323 IDN E7QZ

Name _____ (PLEASE PRINT)

Address _____ Apt. #

City _____ State/Prov. _____ Zip/Postal Code

Signature (if under 18, a parent or guardian must sign)

Mail to **Steeple Hill Reader Service:**
IN U.S.A.: P.O. Box 1867, Buffalo, NY 14240-1867
IN CANADA: P.O. Box 609, Fort Erie, Ontario L2A 5X3

Not valid for current subscribers to Love Inspired Suspense books.

Want to try two free books from another series?
Call 1-800-873-8635 or visit www.morefreebooks.com.

* Terms and prices subject to change without notice. Prices do not include applicable taxes. Sales tax applicable in N.Y. Canadian residents will be charged applicable provincial taxes and GST. Offer not valid in Quebec. This offer is limited to one order per household. All orders subject to approval. Credit or debit balances in a customer's account(s) may be offset by any other outstanding balance owed by or to the customer. Please allow 4 to 6 weeks for delivery. Offer available while quantities last.

Your Privacy: Steeple Hill Books is committed to protecting your privacy. Our Privacy Policy is available online at www.SteepleHill.com or upon request from the Reader Service. From time to time we make our lists of customers available to reputable third parties who may have a product or service of interest to you. If you would prefer we not share your name and address, please check here. ☐

Help us get it right—We strive for accurate, respectful and relevant communications. To clarify or modify your communication preferences, visit us at www.ReaderService.com/consumerschoice.

LISUS10R

HARLEQUIN®

A *Romance*

FOR EVERY MOOD™

Spotlight on

Classic

Quintessential, modern love stories
that are romance at its finest.

See the next page
to enjoy a sneak peek from
the Harlequin® Romance series.

*See below for a sneak peek from our classic
Harlequin® Romance® line.*

Introducing DADDY BY CHRISTMAS by Patricia Thayer.

MIA caught sight of Jarrett when he walked into the open lobby. It was hard not to notice the man. In a charcoal business suit with a crisp white shirt and striped tie covered by a dark trench coat, he looked more Wall Street than small-town Colorado.

Mia couldn't blame him for keeping his distance. He was probably tired of taking care of her.

Besides, why would a man like Jarrett McKane be interested in her? Why would he want to take on a woman expecting a baby? Yet he'd done so many things for her. He'd been there when she'd needed him most. How could she not care about a man like that?

Heart pounding in her ears, she walked up behind him. Jarrett turned to face her. "Did you get enough sleep last night?"

"Yes, thanks to you," she said, wondering if he'd thought about their kiss. Her gaze went to his mouth, then she quickly glanced away. "And thank you for not bringing up my meltdown."

Jarrett couldn't stop looking at Mia. Blue was definitely her color, bringing out the richness of her eyes.

"What meltdown?" he said, trying hard to focus on what she was saying. "You were just exhausted from lack of sleep and worried about your baby."

He couldn't help remembering how, during the night, he'd kept going in to watch her sleep. How strange was that? "I hope you got enough rest."

She nodded. "Plenty. And you're a good neighbor for

coming to my rescue."

He tensed. Neighbor? *What neighbor kisses you like I did?* "That's me, just the full-service landlord," he said, trying to keep the sarcasm out of his voice. He started to leave, but she put her hand on his arm.

"Jarrett, what I meant was you went beyond helping me." Her eyes searched his face. "I've asked far too much of you."

"Did you hear me complain?"

She shook her head. "You should. I feel like I've taken advantage."

"Like I said, I haven't minded."

"And I'm grateful for everything…"

Grasping her hand on his arm, Jarrett leaned forward. The memory of last night's kiss had him aching for another. "I didn't do it for your gratitude, Mia."

Gorgeous tycoon Jarrett McKane has never believed in Christmas—but he can't help being drawn to soon-to-be-mom Mia Saunders! Christmases past were spent alone…and now Jarrett may just have a fairy-tale ending for all his Christmases future!

Available December 2010, only from Harlequin® Romance®.